SNOW PLACE LIKE HOLLY POINTE

CINDY KIRK

WAVERLY
HOUSE

CHAPTER ONE

Lucy Cummings's day began with sunshine streaming through a bedroom window edged in lacy frost. Warm and cozy beneath a thick mound of blankets, Lucy yawned, then rolled over to check the time.

Giving a little squeal, she tossed back the comforter and sprang out of bed. Her normally infallible internal alarm clock had failed her...big-time.

Not even awake five minutes, and she was already behind by ninety. Lucy knew the cause. She'd stayed up late answering emails that her assistant had once covered.

Hedy Sherwood, Lucy's former assistant, had retired in September. After weeks of searching, Lucy had hired Davina Orth last month to replace her. Two days ago, Davina just stopped showing up.

Probably for the best, Lucy told herself as she quickly dressed. Though the young woman had caught on quickly, Davina hadn't been the hardest worker.

As Lucy didn't have time to interview, hire and train someone new, she'd decided to move forward without an assistant and save the salary. The downside of that decision was, instead of spending time with friends over the holidays, her evening hours would be filled with returning calls and answering emails.

For now, priority one was getting enough coffee in her to jump-start her system. Only when she reached the kitchen in her small house on the edge of Holly Pointe did she remember that her coffeemaker had gone to the great appliance graveyard in the sky yesterday.

No problem. She could pivot.

Lucy concluded her luck was on an upswing when she snagged a parking spot in front of the Busy Bean. Then she got close to the coffee shop and saw the line.

Glancing down the street, she considered another option. Rosie's Diner would be busy, too—heck, the place was always hopping—but it was Friday, which meant her friend Mel would be working.

Moments later, Lucy stepped inside the eatery. Her senses were immediately tantalized by the intoxicating aroma of bacon and fried eggs. Her stomach growled.

Though Lucy wished she could sit and enjoy a leisurely breakfast, there wasn't time.

Behind the counter, Melinda Kelly, a pretty woman with thick red hair and gorgeous hazel eyes, stood at the register. She smiled as she handed an older man with thinning brown hair his change. "Please come again."

Mel's attention shifted. Her smile widened when she spotted Lucy. "Hey, girlfriend. This is a nice surprise. I didn't think I'd see you today."

"My coffeepot did a swan dive yesterday, so I decided," Lucy rummaged in the huge bag over her shoulder and pulled out a travel mug, "to swing by for a caffeine fix. Can you help an addict out?"

"I can." Mel nipped the mug from Lucy's fingers. "And I will."

Seconds later, Lucy took her first sip. Not the snickerdoodle flavor she'd planned to get at the Bean, but it would do. Yes, it would most definitely do. She practically inhaled the next gulp and felt almost human as the caffeine jolted her system fully awake.

"What's up? It isn't even eight, and you already look stressed." Concern filled Mel's eyes. "That's a new record, even for you."

Lucy waved a dismissive hand and took another sip. "Stressed is how I roll these days."

"Is the new assistant able to help at all?" Mel pulled her brows together as if trying to recall the girl's name. "Or is she still in training?"

"Davina stopped showing up on Wednesday." Disappointment had Lucy taking another hit of caffeine.

"Is she sick?" Mel asked.

"I don't know what's up with her." Lucy shook her head. "She isn't responding to my calls or texts."

"What are you going to do?"

"I'm done with her." Lucy expelled a breath. "I need someone I can depend on."

"Any prospects?"

"Nope." Though Lucy's voice remained easy, she tightened her fingers around the cup. "I've decided to pick up the slack myself for now and reevaluate after the first of the year."

"You know I'm here for you." Mel reached out and touched Lucy's arm. "I'll help any way I can. Just let me know what you need."

"Thank you." Lucy's voice thickened with emotion. What had she done to deserve such an amazing friend? "But between your day job and helping your mom at the diner, you're on overload, too."

Mel's gaze remained firm. "The offer stands."

"I'll figure it out." Lucy straightened her shoulders. "I've got a great group of employees. While the management tasks might be all mine, I'm definitely not out there alone."

"You'll get it done," Mel assured her. "You're a machine."

"A machine that would function even more efficiently if Davina hadn't bailed," Lucy murmured, wondering even as she spoke why she was giving the young woman a second thought.

"Maybe you'll hear from her today." Mel offered a hopeful smile. "Maybe she'll have a logical explanation for not showing and for ghosting you."

"I doubt it." Still, Lucy pulled out her phone, unable to stop the tiny sliver of hope that surged as she checked her messages. The hope quickly plummeted.

Nothing from Davina. But she saw someone else had been trying to reach her. Seeing the name Paula Franks in her list of missed calls had Lucy emitting a groan.

"Did Davina respond?" Mel leaned across the counter. "What did she say?"

Lucy turned the phone so Mel could read the name. "Zip from Davina. Two missed calls from my mom."

Surprise skittered across Mel's face. "Were you expecting a call from Paula?"

Lucy took another fortifying drink of coffee. The Colombian blend the diner stocked really was good stuff.

"I never expect anything from my mother." As a thought struck her, Lucy couldn't stop smiling. "Still, there is reason to rejoice this morning."

Confusion blanketed Mel's face.

Lucy laughed. "I slept through both of her calls."

Instead of heading straight for her SUV after leaving the diner, Lucy impulsively crossed the street to the town square where the last farmers' market of the year was doing a brisk business.

Lucy smiled as she read the wording on the colorful banners hanging from the ornate light poles surrounding the square.

One, showing a variety of vibrant autumn leaves, simply said

"Kindness," while another with more subdued fall colors urged "Fall in Love with Holly Pointe."

As lovely as these banners were, Lucy knew that immediately after Thanksgiving, the autumn ones would be gone so that Christmas could take center stage.

Lucy remembered when Holly Pointe had started putting up banners. Initially, it had happened only during the Christmas season. Now, banners promoted each season and holiday.

The messaging was always the same—caring and kindness were something to celebrate in this community.

In the square, local growers touted their goods—everything from squatty pumpkins and colorful gourds to a plethora of root crops, such as turnips, beets, carrots and potatoes.

Men, women and children wearing brightly colored jackets shopped under a sky of brilliant blue. The conversation and laughter wafting on the soft breeze wrapped around Lucy like a gentle hug.

Trees continued to lose their formerly brilliant foliage at a rapid pace, their dried leaves making a pleasant crunching sound under Lucy's boots.

A banner strung between two trees proclaimed, "Holly Pointe Has What You Need!"

Underneath, some jokester had planted a homemade sign that said, "If We Don't Have It, You Don't Need It!"

Lucy smiled. Good humor and a strong sense of community abounded in this small town in northern Vermont. As Lucy made a beeline for a stand selling "Cozy Fall Donuts," she reminded herself how blessed she was to live here, to have wonderful friends and to spend her days at a job she loved.

She should already be hard at work, but Lucy shoved away the worry for these few brief moments and basked in the simple joy of being alive on such a beautiful autumn morning.

Up ahead, a sales stand run by Dough See Dough, a local

bakery, was doing a brisk business selling everything from pumpkin streusel to apple pie doughnuts.

Lucy waited in line. When she reached the counter, she smiled brightly. "One apple pie doughnut, please."

Though she couldn't recall her name, Lucy recognized the young woman who took her money as the niece of her third-grade teacher. When Lucy waved away a sack, the woman handed her the doughnut in a paper tissue.

Lucy longed to linger in the autumn sunshine, but duty called.

By the time she had the Barns at Grace Hollow in view, the doughnut was history, her stomach happy and her system well-caffeinated. Lucy slowed the SUV, struck by the sight of the impressive structures nestled between tall pines. Even after all these years, their beauty still stole her breath.

Constructed of reclaimed lumber, stone and steel, the smaller barn housed a chapel with an abundance of stained glass. The Baby Barn, as she lovingly referred to it, was a popular site for intimate weddings, small anniversary parties and other gatherings.

Next to it, rising three stories into the air, the larger one, dubbed the Big Barn, was where larger weddings and events such as the holiday Marketplace were held.

The Barns had been constructed with money Lucy's mother had received in her divorce settlement from husband number four. Paula had modeled these barns after the Big Sky Barn in Texas—which Paula had loved at first sight—building them in Holly Pointe for her foray into event operations.

The construction had experienced numerous setbacks, and Paula's enthusiasm for the project had diminished with each delay and cost overrun. By the time the Barns were ready to open, Paula had lost interest and turned operations over to her daughter.

For her efforts, Lucy received a healthy salary and a

percentage of the profits. The arrangement worked well, especially since Paula kept her distance.

Lucy smiled as she strode toward the buildings, recalling how Mel had once called Paula a thorn in Lucy's side.

Yep, Lucy thought, that pretty much summed up her relationship with her mother.

She'd nearly reached the door when her phone dinged, signaling a text. Lucy had a good idea who it was from.

Pulling her phone out of her coat pocket, Lucy saw with surprise that the text wasn't from her mom, but from Hedy.

Reinforcements on the way. H

Lucy slipped the phone back into her coat pocket and frowned in puzzlement. She wondered what Hedy meant about reinforcements.

Once she made sure everything was flowing smoothly in both barns, Lucy would call Hedy and find out.

The wedding tonight would be an elegant affair with approximately a hundred guests. She'd already checked off the setup for the service in the chapel, as that had been completed yesterday to allow for pictures after last night's rehearsal.

The bride had requested a slight change to the wedding planner's specifications in the reception hall. Lucy checked, pleased to see the change had been implemented.

As she strode past the chapel, Lucy skidded to a stop and blinked. The chairs—covered in white with fancy organza bows in pale teal—had been perfectly arranged last night, but now they were shoved against a far wall. A bucket and a mop sat in the middle of the floor beside a pool of water.

Tipping her head back, Lucy searched the steeply pitched ceiling for the source of the leak. She pulled her phone back out and called the head of her maintenance crew. "Austin. I need you at the chapel. Now."

"If you're calling about the leak, the roof is fixed and shouldn't present any further problems."

"What about this pond in the middle of the floor?"

"I got out the mop and bucket and was going to take care of it, but then I got an SOS from the Big Barn." Stress radiated in Austin's normally calm voice. "Pretty broke out of her pen and was on the loose. She pecked her owner—did quite a number on his arm—but no one else was injured. The boys and me are helping a few irate vendors right stands that were knocked down, and we're cleaning up the floor where the animal took a, well, where she relieved herself."

"I knew letting an emu into the building was a mistake," Lucy muttered.

Despite knowing how temperamental emus could be, Lucy had shoved aside her misgivings when the handler had offered to pay a substantial amount if she'd allow the animal in the vendor's booth that touted the benefits of emu oil. This was one risk that hadn't paid off.

"Like I said, we're in the middle of a mess here, but I can leave now and—"

"No. Stay. Get that mess under control." Lucy slanted a glance at the standing water. "I've got this."

CHAPTER TWO

Lucy pushed up the sleeves of her sweater. She wished for a wet/dry vac, but guessed the one they had was likely in use in the Big Barn.

Thankfully, the mop and bucket were here. Lucy didn't want water sitting on the LVP flooring any longer than it already had.

"Looks like you could use some help."

In the second it took Lucy to turn toward the owner of the deep male voice, the man picked up the mop and went to work.

"Trevor Sherwood." Though it had been over fifteen years since she'd last seen him, Lucy would have known him anywhere.

He flashed a smile, but didn't stop mopping. "Glad you remember."

"What are you doing here?" Lucy knew she should be doing more than simply gaping, but at the moment she couldn't make herself do anything else.

"My grandmother sent me."

Ah, the mysterious text she'd received from Hedy.

After wringing out the mop, Trevor returned to mopping up the water. "If you have towels, now might be a good time to get them. The sooner we get the water off this floor, the better."

Lucy made short work of getting a pile of towels out of the utility room and began sopping up the areas that weren't as deep. With the two of them working together, they quickly cleared the floor of water.

As Trevor wrung out the mop, he glanced over at her. "Do you have a fan?"

"There's one in the utility room." Lucy tossed the words over her shoulder, already headed in that direction.

When she returned, Trevor was wiping down the floor with a dry towel as if wanting to make sure every last drop of water was gone.

"What do you think? Will this work?" Lucy gestured to the industrial fan.

Looking up, Trevor smiled. "Perfect."

She set up the fan, aiming it toward the spot where the water had once stood. "Is the fan really necessary?"

"If this flooring was laminate, I'd say definitely." He studied the floor. "For this vinyl that looks like wood, I'm not sure. Definitely can't hurt."

"Thank you." Lucy glanced at her watch and grimaced. "I'd love to chat, but I need to get these chairs back in place."

Trevor glanced at the chairs. "Tell me where you want them."

Relief surged as she realized he meant to stay and help. Lucy moved to the front of the chapel. "We'll start setting up front to back."

After several minutes, he studied what she'd done so far, and his expression turned puzzled. "What is it exactly we're doing here?"

"It's called a half-circle arrangement." Lucy gestured. "More chairs, please."

As Trevor brought the chairs to her, Lucy spaced them appropriately. Pride filled her with each completed row.

"I thought June was the big wedding month."

Lucy looked up from the chair she'd been placing. "Pardon?"

"Hedy mentioned you've got a ton of weddings scheduled in the Barns from now until Christmas."

She liked that Trevor was cautious in handling the chairs, taking care not to disturb the perfectly folded bow on the back of the fabric that covered each one.

"June weddings are still king, but ever since Holly Pointe was dubbed the Capital of Christmas Kindness, weddings—especially ones in December—have skyrocketed." Lucy basked in the happy thought. "November and December have become nearly as busy as the summer."

"Huh. Never would have guessed." Trevor set down another chair, then glanced around. "That's the last one."

Conscious of the clock ticking down, Lucy pointed to the wooden arch draped with fabric that had been moved to the side. "Could you help me put this back into place? It's kind of heavy."

Not heavy for two, Lucy discovered. Working in tandem, they quickly had it back in position.

Trevor turned to her. "What else?"

"Nothing. Thank you." Lucy pushed back a strand of hair that had fallen into her face. Again. She glanced at her watch. "I'm going to wait a few minutes to put away the fan, then I need to make sure the crisis in the Big Barn is under control."

"Anything I can do to help there?"

"Thank you, but I think it's good." She chuckled. "At least I hope so."

"Sounds like you'll be busy for a while."

Though the warm brown eyes with the thick dark lashes were familiar, his athletic body and his face, with its strong lines and angles, were those of a man, not the boy she'd once known so well.

"There's always plenty to do," Lucy admitted. "But because of your help, this wedding should go off without a hitch."

"I'm glad I could be of assistance." His slightly crooked smile tugged at her memories.

"I'm happy you're back, Trevor." Lucy wished there was time for them to talk. "I don't know how long you're planning to stay, but if it's more than a day or two, I'd love to find a time to catch up."

~

By the time the wedding and reception in the Baby Barn concluded and the Marketplace closed in the Big Barn, it was close to eleven when Lucy walked out the door.

In her arms were several boxes containing Christmas gifts she'd purchased for her friends.

Despite the cold, she left her coat open as she walked to her SUV, relishing the crisp night air. Minus a few anxious moments early on, everything had worked out.

The bride and her mother had been effusive with their praise. In the Big Barn, Lucy had walked the aisles, speaking to the vendors displaying their wares and—other than a few jokes about the emu fiasco—the reports couldn't have been better.

Tomorrow, there were no events scheduled in the Baby Barn. She supposed she should be glad, but empty meant no revenue. If she had any hope of qualifying for a loan to purchase the Barns from her mother at the end of January, she needed every penny of not only her salary, but also the percentage of the profits.

If she didn't get the loan, her mother had indicated she had someone else ready and willing to pay the asking price.

Lucy wasn't certain why her mom was so determined to sell now. Paula insisted she didn't need the money, so why the rush?

She had to admit that her mother did live an extravagant life-style, always jetting off to some exotic destination with a girl-friend or man-of-the-moment. Her divorces had netted her some money, and she took in a tidy sum from the Barns.

"You're out late."

Lucy stumbled back, the gifts in her arms falling to the ground. She whirled, poised to run, but then she heard her name.

"Luce. It's me."

She froze, then slowly turned. "Trevor?"

"Sorry, sorry." He bent to pick up her packages. "I thought you saw me. I didn't mean to frighten you."

"Frighten? You scared me half to death." Her hand rose to her throat as if that gesture alone would be enough to still her racing heart. "What are you doing out here in the dark?"

"I was on my way back to the barns to see if I could find you."

In the glow of the parking lot light, his hair shone like polished walnut. His eyes, well, they'd always reminded her of a chocolate bar, and they still did. A chocolate bar with flecks of gold.

Conscious of his eyes on her, Lucy took the packages from his hands and put them in her car. The simple task steadied her. Turning to face Trevor, she rested her back against the vehicle. "Why?"

"I thought—hoped—we could go somewhere and grab a drink." Appearing unsure for the first time, he shifted from one foot to the other. "Unless, of course, you're too tired or have other plans?"

"No plans." Other than to head straight home. Well, she could be spontaneous. And since it was a Friday night, the bars were open until one. "It'd be fun to catch up."

His mouth lifted in a slow smile. "Where shall we meet? You name the place."

Lucy found that decision didn't require any thought. "Holly Jolly's. Everybody calls it HJ's. It isn't far."

"Just down the road." He nodded. "I saw the sign on my way here."

"The Thirsty Moose and Blitzen's can get a little rowdy, especially on the weekends." The second the words left her mouth, Lucy realized she wasn't being fair. Loud music and wall-to-wall people didn't necessarily constitute *rowdy*. "The truth is, given the choice, I'll always pick HJ's. I think Sam gave this town just what it needed."

"Sam Johnson?"

"Is there more than one?"

Surprise skittered across Trevor's face. "I thought he was mayor or something."

"City administrator. That's his main job. He and his wife, Stella, opened HJ's last year." Lucy smiled, thinking of the brother of her first love, Kevin. "It's very popular with those of us who want to converse with the person we're with without having to shout over the music."

"I remember it was always fun when the Johnson twins were in town." Trevor rubbed his chin. "I can't believe Sam is married."

"For a while now. You were gone a long time." She kept her tone light. "Why was that?"

"I'll tell you over drinks." Trevor flashed a smile. "Good thing we're going someplace where you'll be able to hear me."

Trevor called his grandmother on the way to HJ's to tell her he'd be late getting home. She was spending the evening with Mary Pierson, her friend who owned the Candy Cane Christmas House.

When his grandmother had offered to cancel her plans with Mary, Trevor had told Hedy that her plans for this night had been in the works long before he'd unexpectedly shown up on her doorstep.

They'd already done some talking, but there was more he needed to say to her. Undoubtedly, she had more to say to him. They would have time. Now that he was here, he was in no rush to leave.

Tonight, she would enjoy an evening with her friend, and he would concentrate on Lucy.

He remembered Lucy Cummings as a small blonde-haired girl determined to show that whatever he could do, she could do better.

They'd had a fierce rivalry—and friendship—until he was twelve, and his mother had swooped in and taken him with her to Kentucky. On that day, his bond with Lucy and all his other friends in Holly Pointe had been severed.

On his way to HJ's, Trevor drove past the Thirsty Moose and Blitzen's. From the loud music spilling out into the street, both bars were going strong, even as the midnight hour approached.

Trevor's first impression was that HJ's appeared to be more lounge than bar. With its yellow-and-white-striped awning, green door and acorn string lights around the windows, it was clear this establishment catered to those who preferred a more subdued drinking experience.

Thoughts of Lucy propelled Trevor inside as much as the cold air whipping through a coat that was too light for Vermont in November. Once the door closed behind him, Trevor paused and took stock of the interior.

Sam and Stella had gone for a comfortably rustic look. All walls were brick except for one that was stone and boasted thick mortar joints. Golden flames crackled cheerily in the hearth of a huge fireplace along one wall.

A smile lifted Trevor's lips when he spotted Lucy standing at the shiny mahogany bar, her blonde hair hanging in loose waves down her back.

At Grace Hollow, it had been pulled up in a tail. Though she'd lost the soft, round face of youth and her cheekbones had become more pronounced, she hadn't changed much. He doubted she was much taller than when he'd last seen her. At best, she stood five three.

In the chapel, her eyes had looked bluer to him, but that might have been the lighting. Or maybe they'd always been that vibrant color, and he just hadn't noticed.

Trevor strode to the bar and saw Lucy had already started on a glass of white wine.

"What can I get you?" the bartender asked automatically, then his eyes widened. "Trevor?"

"Derek Kelly." Trevor couldn't stop the grin. "This is a surprise."

Derek chuckled. "More like a shock."

The skinny, sandy-haired boy Trevor remembered had grown up. Derek was close to five ten and had long since left boyhood behind. He had a broad, muscular chest, square shoulders and the battered fingers of a man who worked with his hands.

"When did you get in town?" Derek asked.

"Just today." Trevor couldn't keep the pleasure from his voice. He hadn't been sure if any of his old friends would remember him. "I thought I'd spend the evening with Gran, but she already had plans with Mary Pierson."

"So, you had to settle for Lucy?" Derek dodged Lucy's playful jab.

"Lucy and I have some catching up to do."

"Sorry to interrupt." The female server, dressed all in black, shot Trevor and Lucy a friendly smile before turning to Derek. "Do you have my drink order for table twelve?"

"Coming right up," Derek assured her, then shifted his attention back to Trevor. "What can I get you?"

"Beer. Whatever you have on tap is fine."

Once Trevor had his beer, he and Lucy found a table near the fireplace. The glow from the crackling fire bathed her beautiful face in light. It also emphasized the fatigue that edged her eyes.

"How did things go today?" Trevor took a sip of beer. "Did they get better as the day went along?"

"Well, there were no more water issues in the chapel and no additional bird attacks in the Big Barn, so yes, I'd say things were better." She smiled and lifted her wineglass, clinking it against his pilsner glass. "To old friends stepping up to help."

"It was fun."

She lifted an eyebrow. "Fun?"

He grinned. "I enjoy helping."

"When Hedy texted that she was sending reinforcements, I wasn't sure what to expect," Lucy admitted. "It definitely wasn't you."

Trevor laughed. "It wasn't exactly what I expected either for my first day in town. Hedy told me she feels badly about, as she puts it, 'leaving you in the lurch.' Especially now."

Lucy's expression turned puzzled. "Especially now?"

"The two busiest months of the year." Trevor took a long drink of beer and let himself relax.

Lucy nodded and leaned back in her chair. "We're close to fully booked."

"You're busy. That's what I'm talking about. Hedy feels bad about retiring early—"

"She sent you in her place." Lucy leaned forward again. "I get that, but what I don't understand is, why are you here, in Holly Pointe, at all?" As if hearing the harshness in her own voice, she quickly pressed on. "Don't get me wrong. It's wonderful to see you after so long. It's just that, well, it has been a long time. And," she paused as if considering her next words, "I was under the impression you and Hedy didn't stay in touch."

Trevor took a long sip of his beer and thought about how to reply. He appreciated Lucy trying to be diplomatic even as he missed the boldness of the twelve-year-old girl who'd never feared speaking her mind. Maybe bold was still the way to go.

"Do you remember when we used to talk about what it would be like to have a dad?"

Lucy's eyes grew round as she nodded. "I do. Did you… Did you find yours?"

Being the only child of a single parent was something he and

Lucy had had in common growing up. The fact that he'd lived with Gran and she'd babysat Lucy meant they'd known each other well. They'd shared their worries and their fears with each other.

Trevor hadn't wanted to bother Gran with his fears. She'd had enough to worry about with his mother taking off for long periods of time, sometimes with her friend Paula, sometimes with a guy she'd just met.

Trevor had always been curious about the man who'd paid child support all those years, but never once had tried to contact him. His mother had told him that his dad was a loser who didn't care anything about him.

"I found him."

"Omigod." Lucy leaned forward, blue eyes snapping with excitement. "Tell me everything."

In that moment, Trevor was reminded how she always gave her full attention to whomever she was speaking with.

"My father…" Trevor paused, the words still feeling strange on his tongue. "He's a computer engineer in Seattle."

"Seattle?" Surprise had Lucy's voice rising. "That's about as far from Vermont as you can get."

"Apparently, he and my mom met when she and your mom were partying in Cancun. He was there on spring break. They hooked up during that week, and she wound up pregnant. She contacted him about it, and he paid child support until I turned eighteen."

"Was he certain he was your dad?" As if realizing the implication of what she'd said, Lucy backtracked. "I just meant—"

"He's a smart guy. He asked for DNA confirmation." Trevor's lips quirked upward. "It came back that I'm his kid."

"Did he say why he never came to see you?" Sympathy shimmered in Lucy's blue depths. "Not once in all those years?"

"He said my mom told him she had a steady boyfriend who didn't want him coming around. Later, when I got older and he asked again to see me, she said I didn't want to see him."

"Why would she do that?"

"I can't be sure, but I bet she didn't want him coming around and seeing that she'd dumped me on Gran." Trevor took another sip of beer.

"He could have still pressed. If he was paying child support, he had a right to be a part of your life."

"I know." And when Trevor had looked into his dad's eyes as they'd talked, he'd seen that his dad had known that, too. "At least the guy didn't make excuses when I brought it up."

"I bet he has another family."

"Wife and three kids—two boys and a girl."

"We were unwanted collateral. Both of us."

Like him, Lucy had had no contact with her birth father, the man Paula had married at seventeen. Despite her mother being married three more times after that, none of those men had been interested in taking on a father role for Lucy either.

As far as being *unwanted*, yeah, that word was spot-on.

"We've done okay for ourselves." Trevor thought of his career, one he truly enjoyed. Despite everything that had gone wrong in his life, something had gone right.

"I don't even know what it is you do." Lucy offered an encouraging smile. "Or why you've come back now."

"I came back to see Gran."

"You ignored her for years." There was no censure in Lucy's tone, only confusion. "I never understood why. You loved Hedy. She was more of a mother to you than Angie. None of us understood why your mom took you with her when she married that guy. You had to have been in the way." Lucy's eyes widened as she heard her own words. "I don't mean it was your fault. You were a kid. I just meant that, to Angie—"

Trevor waved her worry away with his hand. "I know what you meant. And I *was* in the way. That is, when she remembered I was there." Trevor took a contemplative sip of beer. "Chad, well, for the most part, he acted as if I didn't exist."

"So why take you?"

Trevor gave a humorless laugh. "From what I've been able to gather, my dad—the one in Seattle—was starting to ask more questions. My mom was afraid if she left me with Gran permanently, and he found out, the child support would stop. I'm not sure if that's how that stuff works, but she was afraid it might."

"Why didn't you tell Hedy how bad it was? She would have come and gotten you in a heartbeat, I know it. She missed you so much. She sent you so many gifts and letters. It never mattered to her that you didn't respond, even though, if we're being honest, I was so angry with you for never..." Lucy's voice trailed off as her gaze searched his face. "You never got them."

"Not a one." Trevor raised the pilsner glass to his lips and took a long drink. Only recently had he learned of Hedy's efforts to stay in touch. "I thought—believed—Gran didn't want anything more to do with me."

"How could you think that?"

"I guess..." Trevor lowered his voice, although there was no one close enough to overhear. "Because it was what I expected, what I'd learned to expect."

Confusion furrowed her brow. "I don't understand."

"Sure you do." He gave a humorless chuckle. "My mom didn't want me. My father sure didn't. The idea that Gran didn't? Well, it made sense to me."

Though she didn't argue, a look of sadness swept across Lucy's face.

"You and me, Luce, we were excess baggage from the moment we were conceived."

His nickname for her might have slipped out, but it sounded right on his tongue. She'd always been Luce to him. Sometimes when he was peeved at her, he'd draw it out—Loooos. She'd acted perturbed, but they'd both known it was only an act.

They'd been buds. The two of them against the world. Both with no father and unwanted by their mothers. They'd bonded over their circumstance in life.

When he'd been stuck in Kentucky, he'd missed Lucy nearly as much as he'd missed Gran. He'd convinced himself they'd both forgotten him. He was beginning to realize now how wrong he'd been.

"What made you come back now?"

"Last call." Derek's voice rang out from the bar.

Trevor considered telling Lucy the whole story, but despite their shared childhood, she was still very much a stranger.

"Short answer?" Trevor downed the last of his beer. "It was time."

Lucy arched a brow. "The long answer?"

"That will have to wait for another day." Pushing back his chair, Trevor held out his hand to her. "Ready to go?"

CHAPTER THREE

Lucy decided her Saturday morning was off to a most excellent start. She beat the rush at the Busy Bean, snagging a primo table by the window. Since her friends had yet to arrive, she sipped her coffee and took out her phone, pulling up the booking schedule for the Barns to review the upcoming week.

She considered a busy November to be the warm-up for a very hectic December. Though Lucy loved everything that went on during these two months, this particular holiday season had her on edge.

The revenue earned during the next sixty days would determine her future. She would put in the work, and if all the stars aligned, the Barns at Grace Hollow would be hers at the end of January.

The purchase price her mother had given her was fair, but not generous.

Then again, Lucy hadn't expected Paula to be generous. In her mother's mind, this was strictly business. Lucy only wished she'd pushed harder for a higher percentage of the profits when she'd first agreed to take over operations at the Barns.

As it stood, she was going to need every penny of the next two months' profits if she hoped to—

"Lucy."

At the sound of her name, she jerked her attention from her phone to see her friend, Kate Sullivan, waving from the counter. Not waving wildly, that wasn't the analytical Kate's style, but just enough to catch Lucy's attention.

Lucy couldn't wait to tell Kate how amazing she looked. This week, Kate had, in her own words, "gone crazy" and had her hair cut in a flouncy collarbone cut, a style that set off her heart-shaped face and her new tortoiseshell cat-eyed frames to perfection.

"They have caramel apple coffee cake," Kate called out. "If I get a piece, will you and Mel help me eat it?"

Lucy gave Kate the thumbs-up. That particular coffee cake, with its layer of Granny Smith apples and streusel topping, was a fall specialty and one of her favorites.

"What's with the thumbs-up?" Melinda, who'd bypassed the coffee line to head straight to the table, dropped her bag onto the floor before settling into the chair opposite Lucy.

"Kate wanted to know if we were interested in sharing a piece of the caramel apple coffee cake."

The laugh that burst from Mel's lips had not only Lucy, but everyone at the nearby tables, smiling. "I can't believe she thought she had to ask."

"I don't think she wanted to be stuck eating it all herself." Lucy took a sip of coffee. "Personally, I can't wait for December. The jingle bell version is my favorite. One of these days, I'm going to remember to ask Norma what she does to give the streusel icing that red cast."

"I asked last year." Kate appeared, placing the coffee cake in the center of the table along with napkins and three forks. "She adds strawberry syrup to the butter."

"I'd never have guessed that." Lucy shook her head, then refocused on Kate. "Love the haircut and the new specs."

"Thanks." Kate smiled at Lucy, her fingers touching her hair before her gaze focused on Melinda. "What's with no coffee? That's not like you."

"I'm working the lunch shift at the diner." Mel offered a good-natured shrug. "All the coffee I want will be at my fingertips."

"I get that," Lucy agreed, then pointed to the coffee cake. "But that practically demands a cup of—"

"This?" Mel pulled a full travel mug from her bag, then glanced furtively at the counter, where the owners, Kenny and Norma Douglas, tended to customers. "Shhh, don't tell on me."

As Lucy made a zipping motion across her lips, she wondered if Mel was having money issues. "Your secret is safe with me."

The three women spent several minutes discussing the weather, munching on coffee cake and enjoying their drinks when Mel fixed her gaze on Lucy.

"A little birdie told me you were at HJ's last night." Leaning forward, Mel lowered her voice as if imparting a great secret. "With a man."

Resisting the urge to roll her eyes, Lucy tapped two fingers against her lips. "Hmmm. Was the little birdie possibly named Derek?"

"You were with a man last night?" Kate set her cup on the tabletop with a clatter. "Who? Do I know him?"

"I don't believe so," Lucy advised, remembering that Kate hadn't lived in Holly Pointe back then. "He's an old friend from childhood. His name is Trevor Sherwood."

"Hedy Sherwood's grandson," Mel supplied. "He went to school with us until he was eleven."

"Twelve," Lucy corrected. "He's here visiting Hedy over the holidays."

"That's cool." Kate pushed her cup aside and leaned forward, her gaze firmly fixed on Lucy. "Is he single?"

Lucy nodded.

"Is he hot?" Kate asked immediately.

"I guess. I mean, you'd probably think he's hot." Lucy thought about Trevor's handsome features and muscular body. "Yeah, I'd say he's hot."

Mel reached over and squeezed Lucy's hand. "When Derek told me about seeing you and Trevor laughing and talking, I found myself thinking how happy that would make Kevin."

Kate shot a sharp glance in Mel's direction. "I thought talking about Kevin was off-limits."

Lucy couldn't hide her surprise. Where had Kate gotten that idea?

Certainly, it had been difficult the first year after Kevin's death to speak of him without crying. But she'd had five years to get her emotions under control.

Kevin, well, he'd been her first. First boyfriend. First lover. First person to breach the carefully guarded wall around her heart.

Though the Johnson family had come to Holly Pointe frequently on vacation, she'd gotten to know Kevin after his parents had purchased a home right outside of town. He'd liked to say she'd captured his fifteen-year-old heart with one smile.

Because of her relationship with Kevin, Lucy had experienced her first real family Christmas. While it was difficult to *not* get in the Christmas spirit when you lived in Holly Pointe, Lucy's mother had always preferred to go somewhere warm over the holidays, preferably without her daughter.

Lucy had jumped at the chance to spend the holidays with Kevin and his family. The year she turned sixteen, they'd celebrated Christmas in New York City, where Kevin's parents, Geoff and Emily, kept a penthouse apartment.

Paula Franks hadn't batted a fake eyelash when Emily— someone her mom had never met—called to ask if Lucy could spend the holiday with them in the city, assuring her mother they would cover all her expenses.

By the time Kevin died, Lucy had spent nine Christmases with the Johnsons and had been embraced by his family as one of their own.

When Kevin passed away from cancer, Lucy had been inconsolable, but she'd soldiered on, knowing that was what Kevin would have wanted. He'd told her exactly that shortly before he passed.

I want you to have a wonderful life, Lucy. I want you to be happy. Find someone who will make you happy, who will make you smile and fill your life with joy. Just make sure he loves Christmas.

Recalling that last caveat always made Lucy smile. She cleared her throat. "There's no reason we can't talk about Kevin."

"Okay, but right now, let's talk about you hooking up with your old friend Trevor." Kate's green eyes sparkled behind her tortoiseshell frames.

"It wasn't a hookup," Lucy protested. "Heck, it wasn't even a date."

"He can't have been in town long, or I'd have heard about it," Mel mused.

"He got in yesterday." The second the comment left her lips, Lucy wished she could pull it back.

"Yesterday?" Mel grinned. "You move fast. Or he does."

"Didn't you hear her? It wasn't a *date*." Kate's hand gave a careless wave. "We both know Lucy doesn't date."

Kate's casual dismissal didn't sit right.

"I date. I mean, I've gone on dates," Lucy countered.

Mel appeared baffled. "Dates? As in plural? Because since Kevin passed, the only one I can recall is that sales guy out of Burlington. That was at least three years ago."

"You're forgetting about the North Country Union High School track coach," Lucy reminded her friend. "That was just last year."

"Actually, two years ago this Christmas, but who's counting?" Mel's soft smile took any edge off the words.

"Both of those dates were pretty much a bust." Lucy took a drink of coffee. "That's why I didn't see either of them again. Not because I'm opposed to dating."

Kate and Mel exchanged a glance, likely thinking of all the times they'd wanted to fix her up this past year and she'd refused.

Mel spoke first. "So, back to your nondate with Trevor."

"Yesterday—at Hedy's request—he stopped by to help me at the Barns. We went out for a drink and conversation after I got off work."

Kate considered, then nodded, appearing satisfied with the explanation. "Like what we're doing now. Drinks and conversation."

"Yes, exactly," Lucy agreed.

Mel drank from her travel mug and said nothing, but the gleam that lingered in her hazel depths told Lucy that Mel was convinced there was more to the story.

"Everyone is talking about the emu fiasco." As if feeling she'd get nothing more from Lucy, Kate changed the subject. "Sounds like Pretty the Emu livened things up at the Marketplace."

Lucy laughed. "That's an understatement."

After discussing the Great Emu Escape, they moved the conversation to tonight's home football game, where the Holly Pointe Hornets would take on their Division III rivals, the Mill River Minutemen.

"Who's going?" Mel gaze swept the table.

"I'm going to try to make it." Kate held up a hand. "No promises. It is, after all, a Saturday night."

Mel's lips lifted in a sly smile. "You're hoping for a better offer."

"A girl can always hope." Kate turned to Lucy. "What about you?"

"I like to attend at least one high school game per season."

Lucy sat back in her seat and considered. "I haven't been this year yet."

"Is that a yes or a no?" Kate asked.

Mel chuckled. "She's hedging her bets, just like you."

Lucy stretched, then glanced at her watch. "I should get to work."

Mel expelled a melodramatic sigh. "Me, too."

"It's Saturday," Kate protested.

"The diner is shorthanded, and weekends are always extra busy. It's the same at Grace Hollow." Despite the comment, Mel remained seated. If she was in a hurry to get to the diner, it didn't show.

Even if Mel hadn't already mentioned working today, the shirt she wore with the diner's logo and the words "Smiles Are Free at Rosie's" was a dead giveaway.

Since Lucy would simply be overseeing the Marketplace today, she'd gone casual with black leggings, boots and a red cable-knit tunic top.

"What's on your agenda today, Kate?" Lucy asked.

"I'm going to do some shopping later. But first I have a quick meeting with Eileen Harbin. You know the Schaefer Brothers purchased the cabins she manages." Kate worked for the family-owned company as a property manager, overseeing a number of rental units catering to tourists. "Hopefully, meeting with Eileen before the property changes hands will ensure a smooth transition."

Lucy thought of the widow who always had a friendly smile and word for everyone. "Eileen has been the caretaker for those cabins as far back as I can remember."

"When Schaefer purchased the cabins after John Rotart passed away, Eileen was given the option to stay on. She thought about it, then declined." Kate's businesslike tone softened. "I'll take over the management of the cabins on January first."

Mel's brows pulled together. "That quickly?"

"Eileen insisted she was ready to retire, but—" Kate hesitated. "I'm not convinced. I think she was scared of dealing with all the changes."

Lucy knew well how difficult change could be. She wondered if Kate was right. Had Eileen decided to retire in order to not have to deal with the demands of a new employer?

"It's good of you to go over and personally discuss the transition." Lucy thought of Eileen, with her tight, tight gray curls and kind eyes. "She's someone who'll appreciate the courtesy."

By the time Lucy and her friends rose to leave, the line at the counter was crazy long. They'd barely taken three steps before their table was cleared, wiped and two couples were sitting down.

Lucy was nearly to the door when she heard Mitch Gardner call her name. She turned back to see him motioning to her.

"You guys have a great day," Lucy told her friends. "I need to see what Mitch wants."

Once she reached his two-top, Lucy braced herself for the diatribe she knew was coming. The guy was never happy. The sun could be shining and he'd complain it was too bright.

"Good morning." Her gaze slid to the empty chair before returning to the skinny man with the sour expression. "Where's Doreen?"

Mitch and his wife participated in the Marketplace every year, doing a booming business selling mittens Doreen made from "upcycled" wool sweaters.

"Where do you think?" Mitch shot her a disbelieving look. "She's working the booth."

Lucy shifted from one foot to the other, somehow managing to keep the bright smile on her face. "Between the Mill River people in town for the game tonight and those who came in early for the leaf-jumping at Hunt's Farm, traffic at the Marketplace this afternoon should be hopping."

"Everything about this season sucks," was his only response.

Lucy really didn't want to get drawn into Mitch's bah-humbug mood. With great effort, she kept the smile firmly fixed on her lips. "Really? In terms of the Marketplace, most everyone exhibiting has reported increased traffic and more sales this year than any other year."

Mitch gave a grudging nod. "Can't complain."

But you will, Lucy thought when he opened his mouth to continue.

"I want you to know I'm still pissed about the Mistletoe Ball being canceled." Mitch's pointy chin lifted in a stubborn tilt.

Lucy's smile slipped, and she resisted the urge to sigh. "Mitch. I explained why the ball had to be canceled. I need to make enough money so I have what I need at the end of January to buy the Barns from my mother. The corporate event I scheduled in place of the ball will give me that money."

"You could have found another way." Mitch gave a derisive snort. "Heck, you could have asked your mom for more time. But no, you had to stick it to the community."

Lucy had asked for more time, but had accepted that her mother was within her rights as a business owner to set the dead-line, especially with another buyer in the wings. Still, it stung that Paula refused to wait even a couple more months when Lucy knew for sure she'd have enough money saved to qualify for a loan.

"I told you before that my mother's deadline is set in stone." Lucy's face felt brittle, as if any second it would crack into a thousand pieces. "I'll miss attending the Mistletoe Ball as much as you—"

"That's a load of crap. If it meant anything to you, you'd find a way to make it happen." He punctuated the words with a stabbing finger. "My wife's been sick this past year. This could be the last year she's well enough to attend the ball."

A headache began to form behind Lucy's left eye. There was no reasoning with this man. It was a waste of breath to even try.

When irritation surged and sharp words hovered on the tip of her tongue, Lucy reminded herself that Mitch might be a curmudgeon, but he adored his wife and was only advocating on her behalf.

Last spring, Doreen had been diagnosed with a serious heart ailment. That knowledge had Lucy swallowing the impulse to strangle Mitch with her bare hands. Instead, she quickly brought the conversation to a close.

Once outside, Lucy took a deep, calming breath and felt herself steady. As she strode down the sidewalk, her thoughts turned to tonight's football game.

The weather would be perfect, at least as perfect as it got for early November in northern Vermont. Had Mel mentioned wanting to go? She should—

"Heads up, buttercup."

The gruff voice had Lucy jerking her head up and pulling her thoughts back to the present.

"I'm so sorry—" she began, then stopped. "Trevor. What are you doing downtown?"

He grinned, and she saw that the top of his ski hat was dusted with snow.

She realized her coat was the same. Snowfall was such a common occurrence during this time of year, it barely registered.

"I dropped Hedy off at Mary's and then stopped in at Rosie's." He took her arm and gently maneuvered them out of the flow of traffic to a spot in front of the antique store Memory Lane. "Mel was coming on duty when I was leaving. It took me a second to recognize her."

"She looks just the same," Lucy insisted.

"What I remember of Melinda Kelly is braces, acne and that she could spit farther than any boy."

"That last one is still true." Lucy laughed. "If spitting were an Olympic sport, she'd be a gold medalist."

"Where are you headed?" he asked.

"To Grace Hollow." She paused and recalled his comment about Hedy. "Wasn't Hedy just at the Christmas House last night?"

"That's right, but apparently there's some apple pie baking contest today, and Hedy is one of the judges."

"But you just got into town." Lucy pulled her brows together. "Couldn't they have found someone to take her place?"

"Hedy and I were both up early and spent some time chatting over breakfast." Trevor waved a dismissive hand. "Since I'll be staying through Christmas, we have plenty of time to catch up."

"Through Christmas?" Lucy couldn't hide her surprise. "That's a long time to be away from home."

He shrugged. "I guess."

She wondered what Trevor did for a living. Likely something to do with computers. He'd always had a quick mind and had been a whiz at all things electronic.

"What do you—?" she began.

"Today, I'm going to help you."

"What? No. Why?"

"Which question to answer first?" He chuckled good-naturedly. "Same song, different verse. Gran feels she let you down by retiring early. If I fill in, she worries less. You get the help that we both know you need, and I feel like a useful member of society and not some guy freeloading off his grandmother."

"You know she doesn't see you that way. None of us do."

"Thank you for saying that." Trevor stepped even closer, turning so his broad shoulders blocked the wind. "Plus, being with her friends makes her happy. Gran is used to a lot of activity, and it sounds like her social life took a hit after she fell and injured her leg last spring."

"But this is your first time back in over fifteen years. Isn't there anything else you'd rather be doing while you're in town? Anyone else you want to see or hang out with?" Lucy met his gaze. "Surely Hedy would understand if you—"

"Let me ask you—when was the last time you talked Hedy out of something once her mind was made up?"

"Fair point."

"Trust me, Luce, there is nothing else I'd rather be doing than spending time with you."

Lucy felt her cheeks warm despite the chilly wind.

"Okay, then." She smiled up at Trevor. "But remember, you asked for it."

CHAPTER FOUR

Trevor strolled beside Lucy as she made the rounds in the Big Barn. She'd been difficult to convince, but she'd finally agreed when he'd insisted that allowing him to help would ease Hedy's mind.

"Who is this young man?" A handsome woman with long silvery hair that lay in a braid down her back looked up from her loom.

According to the signage on her booth, this was Indigo Miller, owner of Sleeping Dogs Twine.

"I'm Trevor Sherwood, Ms. Miller." Trevor didn't extend his hand, since to do so might cause the woman to stop spinning. "What exactly are you making there?"

Trevor had a healthy appreciation for those with a creative passion. When he'd left Holly Pointe, he'd never thought he'd be an artist in the future. Yet, here he was all these years later, with a thriving career he not only loved, but one that brought in a good income.

"I spin dog and cat fur into yarn," Indigo told him, her lips curving upward, obviously pleased by his interest. "I combine the pet fur with a support fiber."

"Why do you do that?" Trevor stepped closer and studied her movements.

"It helps the small quantity of fur become a usable amount of yarn. It also increases the breathability."

"Who knew?" Trevor turned back to Lucy and discovered her watching him. "This is amazing."

"Indigo has been coming to these shows since the Barns were built." Lucy smiled, then motioned to Trevor.

"Before you go, there's something I need to say." Indigo paused her spinning. "I love you, Lucy, you know I do."

Though the smile remained on Lucy's lips, Trevor saw her stiffen. It was as if she knew, as he did, that such a comment usually preceded criticism.

Still, Lucy's expression remained placid, revealing nothing of her inner thoughts. "I'm glad to hear that."

"Getting rid of the Mistletoe Ball…" Indigo shook her head. "It just isn't right."

"You have my word," Lucy lightly touched Indigo's arm, her expression earnest, "the ball will be back next year."

Lucy's promise and her soothing tone did little to staunch Indigo's irritation. A muscle jumped in the older woman's jaw, and she clasped and unclasped her bony hands.

"And what of the people *this year* who will suffer without the financial support the event raises? What about them?" Indigo plowed ahead without giving Lucy the opportunity to respond. "I know some people value big corporations over smaller communities, but that's not how we are here. You should know that." Indigo's shook her head and spoke in a low, cold voice. "You've prioritized money over people, and that's wrong. If Kevin were here—"

"Kevin would understand." Lucy's eyes flashed as if she was challenging Indigo to say differently.

Trevor didn't hear Indigo's response. His mind was mulling the reference to Kevin.

They had to be referring to Kevin Johnson. Unless another Kevin had become part of the Holly Pointe community since he'd left.

Trevor had gotten to know Kevin and his twin when their parents had purchased a farm outside town as a relax-and-recharge oasis from life in the city. Back then, the family had regularly come to Holly Pointe during the holidays and summer.

He hadn't seen either Sam or Kevin since he'd returned.

"Let's go." Lucy motioned for him to follow her.

Trevor saw that Indigo was already chatting up a customer and, from the look of interest on the young woman's face, about to make a sale.

"Was she talking about Kevin Johnson?" Trevor stopped Lucy's forward progress with a hand to her arm. "What did she mean by 'if Kevin were here'?"

"Kevin was crazy about everything Christmas." A distant look filled Lucy's eyes even as her lips curved. "That love included the Mistletoe Ball."

"But where did he go?"

Lucy stared at him.

"It sounds like he left Holly Pointe," he said when she only continued to stare.

"You don't know?" she said at last.

"Know what?"

"Kevin is dead."

Lucy felt good that she'd been able to get the words out. For so many years, she hadn't been able to say them. Or if she did manage to spit them out, the tears would flow with the words.

"Kevin was our age." Shock blanketed Trevor's face. "What happened? Was he in an accident?"

"No accident." Lucy kept her voice even. "Kevin was diagnosed with Hodgkin's lymphoma. He fought hard, but he died five years ago."

"I'm sorry to hear this. Kevin was a good kid."

When she looked into Trevor's eyes, Lucy saw genuine sorrow in the brown depths.

"He was a good kid who grew up to be an amazing man. Smart. Funny. Incredibly kind. And crazy about Christmas." Lucy's laugh was edged with sorrow. She steadied herself, swallowing past the lump in her throat and changing the subject. "It appears everything is working smoothly here in the Marketplace. I have events scheduled in the Baby Barn all week. If you could help me move the chairs, I'd appreciate it."

"Ah, would these be the chairs we set up last night?"

"That would be them." Lucy smiled. "There's a surprise fiftieth birthday party scheduled for tonight."

"In the *Baby* Barn?"

"We only call it that internally. Big Barn and Baby Barn are easy ways for us to differentiate between the two."

"That place is hopping." Trevor shook his head. "A wedding one day and a birthday party the next."

"I wish there was an event scheduled for tomorrow. Any day it sits empty is a day of lost revenue. And you know me, all I care about is money." Lucy swung into her office, where they'd stashed their coats when they'd first arrived, and came out a second later with them. "Once the chairs are put away, there's nothing more to be done."

Trevor took his coat from her. "Luce, don't let Indigo Miller get to you. You're running a business, and that means making hard decisions."

"Right. Yes, I know that. Thank you."

Lucy didn't want to talk about Indigo right now, and she definitely didn't want to talk about Kevin. She wanted to get to work.

For a moment, Trevor looked like he would say more, but then he slipped his arms into his coat. "Okay, then, to the Baby

Barn. Isn't there someone called a day-of coordinator who should have handled the takedown last night?"

"Yes, but when I heard the bride and groom hadn't yet hired a DOC, I said we could do it and at a better price." Lucy studied him. "Not too many men are familiar with DOCs. Unless they've been involved in wedding and reception planning."

"I never made it down the aisle." Trevor shrugged. "But I got close once."

"What happened?" Normally, Lucy wasn't one to pry, but she *was* curious about Trevor's life since he left Holly Pointe.

"My ex-fiancée, Anna Beth, called it off."

Lucy pulled her brows together. "Why did she do that?"

"She had a good reason." His brown eyes turned thoughtful. "Though the whole thing has now taken a crazy turn."

"I like crazy turns." In an attempt to lighten the mood, Lucy shot him an impish smile. "In fact, the crazier the better."

"Then you're going to love this plot twist."

They crossed to the Baby Barn through an enclosed walkway. Through the glass, Lucy noticed that snow fell in large fluffy flakes, whipped lightly by a wind that appeared to be increasing.

When they reached the Baby Barn, they took off their coats and went to work. After a couple of minutes, Lucy paused. "You didn't tell me the crazy story."

Trevor laughed. "I thought you might have forgotten. Or lost interest."

"I'll give you the first, because that might have happened. In terms of the second, you know me better than that." Lucy kept her tone light, hoping Trevor knew she wouldn't judge him.

Only in the last handful of years had she begun to see just how much her past affected the here and now. She wondered if it was the same for him.

Trevor began to stack chairs as he spoke. "Anna Beth and I met in Knoxville. I'd moved there after high school."

"Before that, you lived in Lexington."

"That's right. Lexington is where I lived when my mom took me away from home."

Took me away from home.

Lucy thought it an apt expression since essentially that's what Angie had done. She'd taken her son, the boy she'd never had time for, away from the only home he'd ever known.

"How did you meet Anna Beth? Did you work together?" Lucy prompted when he didn't say more.

"We met at an arts festival and hit it off. We started dating. Things were good." Trevor's gaze turned distant as he looked back. "She wanted the ring and the big ceremony, so I figured okay."

Did he realize, Lucy wondered, that his attitude didn't smack of a man eager to wed the woman he loved?

Lucy wouldn't judge. After all, she'd loved Kevin, but hadn't been able to bring herself to set a wedding date. She offered Trevor an encouraging smile.

"The wedding was set for this coming June. Anna Beth was excited, caught up in all the wedding preparations." Trevor stopped stacking chairs. "I tried to be excited, too. Tasted cakes, visited venues and looked for the right band. But my heart wasn't in it.

"Anna Beth was busy, but she wasn't blind. She could see that something was wrong. At first, we both tried to dismiss it as nerves. I wanted to be the kind of guy who *wanted* to be married. The kind of man who could make a big commitment and see it through. But I think, really, I just didn't want to be like my mother."

"I know your mom, ah, dated a lot of guys before she got married," Lucy said, carefully choosing her words, "but she and Chad have stuck, right?"

Trevor's laugh contained no humor. "She might still be married to Chad, but she hasn't stuck, if you get my drift."

"She isn't faithful to him?"

"Nope. Maybe six months, if that." Trevor lifted one shoulder and let it drop. "Chad's been no better. You could say that in the fidelity department, the two are a perfect match."

"I'm sorry." Lucy placed a hand on his arm. "I hoped she'd changed."

Trevor waved a dismissive hand. "Anyway, I wasn't right for Anna Beth. She wanted a different kind of man. Truth be known, she wasn't right for me either." His eyes took on a faraway expression. "Eventually, she came to me and told me she knew I wasn't in love with her."

"What did you say?" Lucy asked in a quiet voice when he didn't immediately continue.

"I started to deny it, but she was right," he said simply. "I was in love with the idea of being *that* guy."

"I'm sorry, Trev." Lucy scanned his face. "That had to be difficult."

He shrugged.

"You don't seem all that upset about the breakup."

"I feel bad about not being honest with her. In terms of calling off the wedding, well, that was the greatest gift she could have given both of us. She deserved better than a guy who was just going through the motions."

"We all deserve that." Lucy thought of the two men she'd dated recently. The worst thing she could have done was go out with them again when she wasn't interested. "What's the plot twist?"

Trevor's lips curved. "She and her old boyfriend got back together and are planning to get married on the date we'd chosen."

"No way!" Lucy's eyes widened. "That's crazy."

Trevor grinned. "It just proves the old saying is true—when you know you know." Still smiling, he met her gaze. "What about you? Did you ever take a trip down the aisle? Or come close?"

How much to say? Lucy thought, then she realized she might as well tell him. If he spent any more time in Holly Pointe, he'd hear it all anyway.

"Kevin Johnson and I were exclusive from the time we started dating at fifteen until he died." Lucy kept her tone even. "We were in college when Kevin proposed, and I accepted. I loved him with my whole heart. When they lowered him into the ground, my heart went with him."

Trevor's expression turned solemn. "Yet, you were together all those years and never got married."

Though it wasn't a question, Lucy felt compelled to answer. "I liked the way things were."

"Did he like your arrangement?"

Lucy shifted uncomfortably. She could say yes or hedge, but she went with full honesty instead. "Kevin and I talked about getting married right after college graduation. But we were so young. My mom married young, so maybe that was in my head. I didn't want to make the same mistakes she did."

"How could marrying the man you love ever be a mistake?"

Lucy had no answer for the question she'd asked herself many times.

"I know we'd have eventually married." Lucy briefly closed her eyes. "Then Kevin got sick, got better, got sick again." She blew out a long, shaky breath before adding, "Then he died."

"I can't imagine how difficult that was for you." Trevor expelled a breath. "I didn't realize…"

"There was no way you could know," Lucy told him. "There hasn't been anyone else since. I've gone on a couple of dates, but Kevin, well, he's a hard act to follow. I'm okay being alone."

She sensed him studying her, his expression unreadable.

"Not to change the subject…" he began.

"Please do." She shot him a grateful smile.

"What did Indigo mean when she said people would suffer without the financial support the Mistletoe Ball raises?"

For Lucy, this had been one of the hardest parts about

canceling the ball. She rested her back against the cart holding stacks of chairs. "Each year, ninety percent of the profits are donated to the University of Vermont Cancer Center with the other ten percent going to fund local health care needs."

"Since that's a hundred percent, then you don't make anything when you host the ball." Trevor said it as a statement.

"That's correct." She lifted her hands. "But that's okay. Well, most years it's okay. This year, I need the revenue, and I was able to book a corporate event for that weekend, so that's what I did."

"You're a business owner." Trevor offered a supportive smile.

"Some people think I'm being heartless."

"Anyone who knows you—really knows you—wouldn't believe that for a minute." The look in his eyes was as warm and steady as the clasp of his hand on her shoulder. "Let's get to work."

Lucy turned to push the cart holding stacks of chairs, but found it heavier than she'd thought. No wonder she normally left this task to Austin and his crew.

When she turned to Trevor, she found him smiling.

"Need help?"

She smiled back. "Maybe just a little."

In an instant, he was beside her, his strong hands next to hers. With both of them pushing, the cart rolled easily.

"Where are we taking this?" he asked.

"Into the back." She lifted one hand and pointed. "Through those doors, just keep going straight."

"Why don't you open the doors, and I can push this through?"

"Are you sure you can handle it on your own?"

He grinned. "It won't be easy, but I'll manage."

In a matter of minutes, all the chairs were stowed. Hands on hips, Lucy surveyed the room. "The cleaning crew will be in to make sure everything is spotless, but now we're ready for them."

"What else can I do to help?"

Lucy realized with a sudden pang that her work here was done. "I believe that's it."

"Do you have plans for tonight?"

The question took her by surprise. "I've thought about going to the Homecoming game at the high school, but I may just go home. I'm not sure."

Trevor's gaze grew watchful. "If you did go, who would you go with?

"Myself." She smiled. "I'm pretty good company."

"Yes, you are."

Lucy couldn't stop the flush of pleasure at his words.

"I'm going to the game tonight, and I'm passable company." He smiled and cocked his head. "What would you think about going together?"

CHAPTER FIVE

Lucy shoved her mittened hands into the pockets of her ski jacket. The wind had picked up since she and Trevor had left the truck to head to the stands.

The crowd surrounding them blocked much of the breeze. Lucy slanted a glance at Trevor. For someone who lived in a Southern state, he appeared to have acclimated well to the cold. Likely due in no small part to a coat that appeared arctic-rated.

"Is that jacket new?" She would have sworn the one he'd worn last night had been blue.

"It is." He flashed a smile. "The coat I brought with me just wasn't cutting it. Fine for temps in the forties, but below that…"

"I like this one on you." She scanned down, taking in the worn jeans and hiking boots, then returning her gaze to his face and those deep-brown eyes. "That caramel color looks good with your eyes."

Lucy flushed. While that might be something you'd say to a girlfriend, it wasn't a compliment you'd normally give a guy who was only a friend.

"Caramel, huh?" Trevor glanced down then back at Lucy. He

shrugged. "The clerk told me it was utility brown, but I think I like caramel better."

"Do you like football?" Lucy decided to forgo any more discussion on clothing.

"Doesn't everyone?" Trevor glanced at the stadium, with its wooden seating on one side of the ball field. "What about you?"

"Well enough." Lucy gestured to the high school building off to their right. "I'm here mostly just to support the community and the high school. I have many fond memories of my years there."

"Let me guess." Trevor's studied her face. "You and Kevin were Homecoming king and queen?"

Lucy laughed. "That was so long ago."

The memory of standing on that ball field, her arm looped through Kevin's while they were crowned, was a sweet one that she'd never forget.

"How was your high school experience?" Lucy asked, realizing they spent too much time talking about her and not about him. "You went to high school in Lexington?"

"I did." He shrugged. "It was a big school."

"How big?"

"Over two thousand in grades nine through twelve."

"That is big." She started to comment on how many had been in her class at Holly Pointe—or rather, how few—but stopped herself. This was about him, not her. "Did you like it?"

"I did. You could be as involved as you wanted to be."

"Were you involved?"

"Most of the activities cost money to participate." Trevor held up a hand when Lucy started to speak. "That was okay. Since my mom and Chad liked to keep any of their extra money for themselves, I worked during high school. Having a job doesn't leave time for sports."

"I'm sorry." Pulling her hand from her pocket, Lucy touched the sleeve of his coat.

"Don't be." He sounded surprisingly sincere. "I had friends, a job that paid okay and lots of freedom. Some would say I had it made."

"Would you like to buy a wreath?"

Lucy turned at the sound of the familiar voice.

Camryn Kelly, wearing a bright-yellow-and-black-striped ski cap, held up a picture of an evergreen Christmas wreath that sported a red velvet bow. "We're selling these to raise money for a drama club trip to New York City next spring. They're very nice and will brighten the exterior of any home."

The canned speech nearly made Lucy smile. But she'd participated in enough of these fundraisers growing up to know just how much getting an order meant.

"Trevor." Lucy turned to him, gesturing toward the girl. "This is Camryn Kelly, Derek's daughter."

"Nice to meet you." Trevor smiled. "Your dad is good guy."

"He is." Camryn flashed a smile. "Dad bought a wreath. He knows they're a great deal."

"You've convinced me," she told Cam. "I'll take two."

"Two?" Cam's expression brightened. "You want two?"

"I do." Lucy cocked her head. "Do I pay now or—?"

"You'll pay when they're delivered, which will be on December first."

Lucy smiled. "Perfect timing."

"We thought so." Cam's face took on an earnest expression. "Most people like to do their decorating right after Thanksgiving."

"I'll take one," Trevor said, surprising Lucy.

Lucy turned to him, and he must have seen the question in her eyes.

"For Hedy," he said.

Camryn's pencil hesitated on her order sheet. "Hedy Sherwood?"

"She's my grandmother," Trevor told the girl. "I'm Trevor."

"That's nice of you." Cam's smile flashed, then she looked down and added his name before looking up again. "Thank you both for the orders."

"Hope you sell a ton of wreaths tonight." Lucy smiled.

"Going good so far." Cam turned to a group of middle-aged couples, and her eyes lit up. "They look like wreath people."

Trevor chuckled. "Good luck."

Cam wriggled her fingers and headed straight for the couples.

"I can't believe Derek has a kid that old." Trevor shook his head as they watched her approach the group.

"He's done a great job raising her on his own."

"What about her mother?" Trevor stopped. "Is it anyone I'd remember?"

"Elin Daniels?"

"Doesn't ring any bells."

"She and Derek were hot and heavy during high school." Lucy considered how much to tell, but it wasn't like any of this was a secret. "Elin got pregnant junior year. She continued the pregnancy, but didn't want to keep the baby. Derek did."

"That had to be difficult."

Lucy thought of all the ways it was difficult, but went with the one he likely meant. "Derek continued in school, but quit sports. Rosie was willing to help him out by watching the baby while he was in class, but otherwise, Cam was his responsibility."

"Wow." Trevor shook his head. "What about Elin?"

"She and her family moved from Holly Pointe. She signed over all rights to Camryn when she was a baby."

"Does she come and see her?"

"She signed over all rights," Lucy repeated.

"That just gives him full custody." Trevor glanced toward the field at the sound of the marching band. "It doesn't mean she can't see her daughter."

"From what I understand, Elin isn't interested in pursuing a relationship with her daughter."

"Her loss," was all Trevor had to say as his eyes zeroed in on a hot dog vendor just outside the entrance to the stadium. "Want a hot dog?"

Lucy grinned up at him. "Do you really have to ask?"

∼

Trevor wondered how he could have forgotten Lucy's love of hot dogs. As Hedy considered hot dogs to be junk food, Lucy's love of them as a little girl and desire to eat them constantly had put her and his grandmother at odds.

"I restrict myself to one a week." Lucy bit into the hot dog. "I've found if I eat healthy, I have more energy and feel better."

"Well, I guess tonight I'll have to deal with sluggish Lucy."

"Can't blame tonight on the hot dog." Lucy finished off her dog. "I was tired before I even came to the game."

"We don't have to stay for the entire game—"

"Hey, nobody leaves a Hornets game early. Even if they're way behind, we stay and cheer as the team leaves the field."

When he saw that she was serious, he only smiled.

He'd forgotten much of what it was like to live in a small community. Trevor had wondered how it would feel being back in Holly Pointe after all these years away.

The town was the same in many ways, but different. Most of the time, he felt like an outsider. Unless—he slanted a glance at the woman beside him wiping mustard from her lips with a paper napkin—he was with Lucy.

When he was with her, he felt part of the community he'd left behind all those years ago.

"Ready to climb?" she asked, pointing to the steps leading to the upper bleachers.

"Let's say hello to Gran and her friends first," Trevor suggested, gesturing with one hand.

Lucy's expression brightened. "Hedy is here?"

"She is." Trevor took Lucy's arm, steering her lightly down the sidelines, behind the team benches. "She was happy to hear we were both going to be here tonight. Apparently, she's part of some senior cheer squad, and she wanted me to see her perform."

"The Galaxy Gals." Lucy chuckled. "I forgot all about that group."

"Are they any good? She didn't really go into detail about what they do."

"Just wait until halftime," Lucy told him. "You can see for yourself."

Spotting Hedy up ahead, Lucy increased her pace.

Trevor hurried to catch up.

By the time he reached his grandmother, Lucy had already flung her arms around Hedy.

"It's been too long," he heard Lucy say.

"I'm so glad to see you." Hedy's arms tightened around Lucy. "You're right. It has been too long."

Only when Hedy released Lucy did she appear to catch sight of Trevor.

Hedy opened her arms. "I've got a hug for you, too."

When Hedy pulled him close, Trevor realized just how much he'd missed her hugs.

"You be good to my Lucy," she murmured.

"Hey, what about telling her to be good to me?" Trevor teased as his grandmother held him at arm's length.

Looking at Hedy, Trevor could see where his mother got her dark hair and brown eyes. But that's where the resemblance ended, at least as far as Trevor was concerned. Hedy's open and friendly expression and kind eyes had little in common with his mother's cynicism.

Angie always seemed to be trying to figure out how she could use someone for her own gain, which was why Trevor had little contact with her.

"You two best be finding your seats," Hedy warned. "Looks like there's going to be a full house tonight."

Trevor and Lucy found seats near the top. They'd just sat down when Derek appeared and squeezed in on the end next to Lucy.

Derek clapped his mittened hands together. "Should be a good game."

Trevor leaned forward. "I thought you'd be bartending."

For a second, Derek looked confused, then he grinned. "I was filling in last night."

"We ordered some wreaths from Cam," Lucy told Derek.

"I appreciate it." Derek offered a rueful smile. "That trip to New York won't come cheap. I—"

Whatever he was about to say was cut short when a roar went up from the crowd as the Hornets took the field. Trevor stood and cheered along with the rest of the Holly Pointe fans in their section.

During the first half, there wasn't much conversation from Lucy or Derek. Both, it appeared, took their football seriously. Trevor didn't mind. He was content with soaking in the sights and sounds of small-town life.

Before returning to Holly Pointe for this visit, he'd convinced himself that he couldn't live without all the amenities found in a large city. The cold, well, that was one thing he was certain he didn't miss.

But now, sitting in the stands, with the temperature cold enough that he could see his breath, it didn't seem such a big deal.

The coat made a difference, he knew. But it was—

Lucy's elbow in his side got his attention. She pointed. "The Galaxy Gals are taking the field."

"Let's give a warm welcome to Holly Pointe's own senior cheer squad, the Galaxy Gals."

Whistles, cheers and clapping swept through the stands as the nine women moved to the center of the field. They were dressed identically in red jackets with silver trim. Each carried a pair of red and silver pompoms.

From where he sat, Trevor had difficulty recognizing the person who appeared in charge of the squad.

"Who is the captain?" Trevor asked.

"Ginny Blain." Lucy spoke without taking her eyes off the women.

"Shawn's mom." Trevor struggled to bring back memories. "There was another brother."

"Spencer," Derek supplied.

"Now I remember."

At that moment, Trevor heard Ginny yell out, "Ready?"

The fact that he could hear her at all this far up told Trevor that Ginny must be wearing a microphone.

The women around her lifted their pompoms in unison and yelled, "We've got razzmatazz."

Trevor couldn't pick up the other words, though he thought he heard *pep* and *pizzazz* as the women dipped, swayed and turned in unison, pompoms flashing through the air.

The cheer ended with the women and the crowd shouting, "Razzmatazz."

The smile on his grandmother's face brought a thickening to Trevor's throat. When he'd discovered what his mother had done when she'd whisked him away from Holly Pointe, his concern had been for his grandmother. She'd been left alone.

Only now did he realize how ridiculous his concern had been. Hedy might not have any family in Holly Pointe, but she definitely wasn't alone.

"Wasn't she great?" Lucy's eyes shone, and her lips looked as red as ripe strawberries.

"Amazing," Trevor agreed, having difficulty pulling his attention from her lips.

"When she injured her knee, it killed her to back away from the Galaxy Gals." Lucy smiled. "I'm so happy she's back at it."

"My mom told me they all missed her," Derek commented.

Trevor pulled his brows together. "Hedy told me her injury was last spring. There wouldn't have been any football games then."

"Oh, the women don't just perform at high school sporting events. They perform at senior centers and special events in the area as well as march in parades," Lucy explained.

Derek chuckled. "From the look on your face, this is all news to you."

"I've been away awhile." Trevor could feel Lucy looking at him.

"Why was that?" Derek asked.

"Long story." Trevor pointed to the field. "Looks like they're ready to crown the Homecoming royalty."

Trevor didn't know any of the kids on the field, but he applauded with the rest of the Holly Pointe fans at the ceremony.

Out of the corner of his eye, he saw Lucy watching the events on the field, her expression unreadable. He didn't need to be some sort of psychic to know that she was thinking of Kevin, no doubt recalling how it had felt when the two of them had been on the field.

Derek's expression was equally inscrutable. From what Lucy had said, he'd already been responsible for the care of a baby his senior year. Was he thinking of that year and how different it had been from what he'd probably imagined it would be?

It reminded Trevor of what Ray, his neighbor and the finest man he'd ever known, would tell him when he'd complained about his life. "Trevor," he'd say, "Everyone is fighting battles you know nothing about."

Looking back, Trevor realized that while his life had been no cakewalk, it could have been far worse.

The second half of the Homecoming game went quickly, with the lead going back and forth, until the Hornets pulled out a win with a last-second field goal.

Everyone, including Trevor and Lucy, was in high spirits as they descended the steps. Derek left to meet up with Camryn.

That was okay with Trevor. He liked being alone with Lucy, even surrounded by hundreds of football fans.

"Where to now?" he asked.

"What would you think about checking out the party in the high school gymnasium?"

"Isn't that just for the high school students?"

Lucy had already started walking toward the high school, so Trevor fell into step beside her.

"The Homecoming dance for students was last night," Lucy explained. Sensing his confusion, she continued, "It's not the way things used to be done, but about five years ago, the town decided to embrace the idea that 'everyone is a Hornet' on Homecoming Saturday."

"How does that work?"

"Well, for starters, the game is on Saturday rather than on Friday night. And no matter if you're from the opposing team or just in town visiting, you're an honorary Hornet, and you're invited to the dance at the high school." Lucy turned. "It's really pretty fun, even though no alcohol can be served in the gym. Word is that the band they booked for this year is amazing."

"I'm up for it," Trevor told her. "Sounds like it could be fun."

As he and Lucy made their way to the gym, Trevor imagined Lucy in his arms as they swayed together to a romantic ballad.

Yes, Trevor thought, he was looking forward to partying in the school gym.

CHAPTER SIX

Music spilled from the exterior doors of the gymnasium. Lucy found her hips swaying to the pulsating beat. When she gave Trevor a hip bump—just because she felt like it—and he glanced over at her, she flashed an impish smile.

"I don't know if it's the cold air or the music, but suddenly I feel as if I could party the night away." She couldn't, of course. Tomorrow might be Sunday, but it was another workday.

She wouldn't think of that now. Tonight, she would enjoy the music and being surrounded by people she knew and loved.

Without warning, Trevor took her hand and gave her a twirl.

Lucy laughed. "What was that?"

"Just getting warmed up."

"I don't know how to tell you this," even as she spoke, laughter continued to run through her voice like a pretty ribbon, "but I don't think that's the kind of dancing we'll be doing."

Trevor's dark eyes gleamed with good humor. "I guess we'll see."

Greeters stood at each door. She saw Sam and Stella at the single door to the far right.

Without thinking, she grabbed Trevor's hand. "Let's go in this door. There's two people I'd like you to meet."

Trevor came willingly, his gloved hand wrapping around her mittened one. She skidded to a stop in front of her friends.

"Lucy." Stella, a willowy brunette, stepped forward for a hug, forcing Lucy to drop Trevor's hand.

For the best, Lucy told herself. She and Trevor were just friends. She wouldn't want anyone to get the wrong impression.

Sam came next, squeezing her tight. "Stella and I were just talking about how we haven't seen you much. You're still coming to Friendsgiving on Friday?"

"As long as nothing blows up at Grace Hollow, I'll be there." Lucy gestured to the man at her side, who'd silently watched the greetings. "Stella, I'd like to introduce you to Trevor Sherwood. He's Hedy's grandson and back in Holly Pointe visiting her over the holidays."

Stella smiled brightly. "It's a pleasure to meet you, Trevor. Hedy is a wonderful woman."

"She's the best." Trevor turned to Sam. "I don't know if you remember me—"

"I do." Sam studied Trevor's face as if trying to reconcile the man who stood before him with the boy from all those years ago. "It's been a long time."

"It has." Trevor's expression turned serious. "Lucy told me about Kevin. I'm sorry, man. Your brother was a good kid."

Sam slanted a look at Lucy as if surprised she'd told Trevor about Kevin. Which didn't make sense at all. Who better to tell Trevor than her?

"Are you two…" Sam gestured vaguely from her to Trevor.

"Going to enjoy the Homecoming party?" Trevor flashed a smile. "I hope."

"It's always a good time. There's nothing that this town loves more than a community dance." Stella's smile extended to both of them. "With the Mistletoe Ball on hiatus this year, I think we're seeing more than normal here tonight."

Lucy flinched. She couldn't help it. She knew Stella hadn't meant anything by the remark, but Lucy found she was extra sensitive after her interactions with Mitch and Indigo.

"Well, it was great meeting you, Stella, and seeing you again, Sam, but it appears we're holding up the line." Trevor laid a hand on Lucy's shoulder. "Ready to show me just what this party is all about?"

Lucy glanced back and saw that Trevor was indeed correct. Even though this wasn't the main door, people were queuing up behind them.

"I'll see you both Friday," Lucy told the couple, suddenly conscious of their curious gazes.

She waited to take Trevor's arm until they stepped inside, then tugged him toward the coat check.

Cam's drama club classmates were working the counter, trying, like Cam, to raise money for the trip next spring.

Lucy watched Trevor slip off his jacket, stuff his hat and gloves into his pocket and hand it to the girl along with a ten-dollar bill.

Trevor gestured to Lucy, who'd just removed her ski coat and hat. "That's for both of us."

"You didn't need to do that," Lucy protested, slipping the mittens into her pocket and handing the young girl her coat.

"Do you want one coat check number or two?" the girl asked.

"You can put them together," Trevor told her, then looked at Lucy for confirmation.

"Yes, that works." She wasn't sure what to think about Trevor's take-charge attitude.

He wasn't overpowering, just confident and sure. Just like her.

Lucy fluffed her hair with her fingers and let her gaze sweep the large room.

"Okay, so tell me what's what." Trevor offered her an easy smile.

He really did have a nice smile, Lucy thought, and found herself smiling back.

"Okay, if you're a graduate of Holly Pointe High, there are round stickers with numbers on them on that table over there." Lucy pointed to a rectangular table on the far side of the gym, "If you graduated in 2020, you could—if you wanted—grab a sticker that has the number twenty on it to show others you graduated from here and in what year."

"What would be the point?" Trevor pulled his brows together. "The school isn't that big that you wouldn't know who graduated with you."

"Conversation starter for those who aren't from here." Lucy shrugged. "It was something the Homecoming Planning Committee started last year in the hopes of helping locals and tourists interact."

"Are there a lot of tourists around in November?"

"More than you'd think." Lucy thought of what Eileen had told her when they'd talked last summer. "The majority of the cabins are already booked for October through December by the beginning of the summer."

"Wow. That's great for Holly Pointe."

"The merchants depend on the tourist dollars. That's how we're able to have so many big-city offerings in such a rural community." Lucy smiled. "Anyway, they want everyone to inter-act, and the stickers are one way to facilitate that. I have no idea if it's working. I heard they're going to take another look at it and see if it's worth continuing."

"What do you think?"

Lucy scrunched up her nose and shrugged. "I don't know. Maybe it works. That's for the committee to evaluate and decide."

She'd already had too many people second-guessing her deci-sions on the Barns to do that to someone else.

Trevor pointed toward the opposite wall. "What are those tables for?"

"Silent auction. Some of the offerings are specifically geared toward tourists, like cabin rentals, while others are just things anyone would enjoy."

"What happens to the money raised?"

"The committee made a decision to have it go toward health care needs in the community, since—"

"Since they won't be getting money from the Mistletoe Ball."

Lucy nodded. She realized she was tired of talking and thinking about the committee's strategy—actually about any business-related concerns.

"Let's dance."

Trevor smiled. "I thought you'd never ask."

Trevor took Lucy's arm as they wove their way through the hordes of people. A lot of them spoke to Lucy, but while she smiled and returned their greetings, she didn't stop to chat.

That was okay with him. Right now, Trevor found himself overwhelmed by the sheer number of people he didn't know. He wasn't sure what he'd expected. Though he'd grown up in this community, he'd been away for over fifteen years.

He'd been a kid when he left. Even his friends, Derek and Sam, while friendly, seemed more like strangers. Only Lucy was different.

Trevor smiled at her determined expression as she led him toward the dance floor. With her, he felt comfortable. With her, he felt as if he'd come home.

He was glad that she was letting him tag along with her. From what he'd picked up from her friends, that was unusual.

When they reached the dance floor, the band of former high school students was rockin' the gymnasium. Trevor wasn't the greatest dancer, but he could move to the beat. He let the pulsating rhythm envelop him and forgot everything in the joy of the moment.

Lucy caught his eyes, and they exchanged a smile as they let the beat flow through them. By the time the set ended, Trevor felt as if he'd run a marathon with no training.

He laughed at how out of breath he felt, somewhat consoled by the fact that he didn't appear to be the only one. As if the band members sensed a mass exodus for refreshments was imminent, they launched into a slow set.

Trevor inclined his head. "Do you want to keep dancing or grab something to drink?"

Lucy appeared to consider, but only for a second. "Let's stay and dance some more."

When she placed her hands on his shoulders, he wrapped his around her and pulled her close. It was warm in the gym, but nothing compared to the warmth her body generated.

Trevor had to fight the urge to brush his lips across her hair, to run his hands up and down her back, and when she tipped her head back and smiled, well, kissing her wasn't the only thing on his mind.

"This is nice," she said, still gazing up at him. "It's been so long that I—"

Giving in to the impulse, Trevor leaned down and brushed his lips lightly across her mouth.

Her eyes widened.

"Thank you." He spoke softly as they continued to sway to the melody of love.

Confusion filled her blue eyes. "For what?"

"For taking me under your wing." With one gentle finger, Trevor tucked a stray strand of hair behind her ear. "For making me feel a part of a community that I deserted all those years ago."

"Not your choice," she reminded him.

"Still happened." He searched her face. "So, thank you."

A soft look filled her eyes. "You're welcome."

He tightened his hold on her, and when she rested her head against his chest, he felt as if he really was home.

~

Trevor dropped Lucy off at her house. It was a small bungalow with a high-pitched roof, a porch across the front and an attached single-stall garage. Painted white with a green roof and green shutters, it reminded him of a dollhouse.

It certainly wasn't much bigger than one.

He pushed his car door open, intending to walk her to her front door, but she placed a hand on his arm and told him to stay put. Trevor didn't back out of the driveway until she was in the house with the door shut and the light on.

Though he told himself he hadn't expected her to ask him inside, he'd hoped.

Lucy remained front and center in his thoughts even when he stepped inside his grandmother's house.

He found Hedy at the kitchen table, drinking a cup of tea. She looked up and lifted her cup when he walked into the room. "Will you join me?"

"I'd love to." He motioned her down when she started to rise. "I can get my own tea. You rest. You expended a lot of energy on that field tonight."

Hedy laughed. "It felt good being back with the squad."

Trevor turned on the burner beneath the teakettle, then returned to the table. "I bet they missed you."

"Not half as much as I missed them." Hedy took a sip of tea. "My knee injury last spring wasn't horrible, but after being on my feet most days, I needed to put my foot up and rest when I got home from work."

The kettle whistled, and Trevor made his tea, bringing it to the table and taking a seat.

"Is that why you retired?" Trevor took a sip of the Sleepytime tea his grandmother preferred in the evening. He couldn't imagine that Lucy wouldn't have been accommodating, but then he remembered how hard she pushed herself. "You couldn't keep up?"

"Lucy was very understanding. That girl went out of her way to help me." Hedy's lips lifted in a little smile. "After my injury, I just didn't seem to have the same amount of energy. I don't need a lot, and with my Social Security, I get by just fine."

"If you need anything—" Trevor began, but the warning look Hedy shot him had him swallowing the offer.

He knew his grandmother to be a proud woman, and he respected that. He would also do whatever he could to make her life easier.

"This is a busy, busy season at Grace Hollow. My leaving wasn't great timing, but Lucy has never made me feel guilty. I love her for that." Hedy met his gaze. "That's why I'm happy you're here and that you've agreed to help her."

"I like helping Lucy." He'd managed to keep his tone offhand, but Trevor couldn't stop the smile. "She's amazing."

"That she is."

"I hate that you and I spent so many years apart." Though Hedy was still a vibrant woman, she'd aged considerably in the years he'd been gone.

She was his family, really his only family, and she wouldn't be around forever.

Reaching out, Hedy covered his hand with hers. "What I wouldn't have given to have my Angie say that just once to me."

"Gran—"

Hedy's eyes grew soft. "We're both busy, active people. You and I are going to spend plenty of time together over the next two months...and I'm going to enjoy every minute."

"Whatever you need—"

"You're already giving me what I need by helping Lucy.

Knowing you're helping her at Grace Hollow, even seeing you two in the stands having fun, well, that's what I need." Leaning forward, Hedy cupped his face with her hand. "I love you, Trevor, and I'll be honest. I love seeing you becoming involved in the community. My hope is you may end up liking it here so much, you'll never want to leave."

CHAPTER SEVEN

Trevor saw Lucy every day of the following week. He helped out at Grace Hollow, doing everything from responding to emails requesting pricing and more information about Barn amenities, to making sure the people associated with the scheduled events had everything they needed.

He enjoyed working side by side with Lucy. His favorite days were ones when they worked together to complete a task or the ones when they grabbed a quick lunch, put up their feet and talked while they ate.

Lucy had endless energy and an upbeat spirit. The only time he'd seen her upset was on Wednesday when her mother called. Though Lucy had gone in the office to take the call, by the time she'd come out, the spark that he'd seen in her eyes moments earlier had vanished.

Tonight, she was in high spirits when they left Grace Hollow for a Friendsgiving dinner party.

Trevor glanced down at this flannel shirt and jeans. "Are you sure I didn't need to go home and change?"

Normally, he didn't pay a lot of attention to what he wore, but what he'd put on today to help Austin and crew move some booths seemed extra casual.

"You look fine," Lucy said without glancing in his direction. "I'm just wearing what I had on today."

He thought about mentioning that was an unfair comparison because she looked amazing in a plaid wraparound dress with boots. She looked like a woman attending an early Thanksgiving event with friends.

He looked like the guy who should be bringing in firewood and shoveling snow from the walkways. But he said nothing more. All that mattered was that he would be spending the evening with Lucy.

Trevor realized, as he glanced at the snow-covered fields they passed by, that this road was familiar. He'd been to the farmhouse outside Holly Pointe numerous times with Sam and Kevin.

He'd loved the rambling farmhouse, and he recalled how welcoming Mr. and Mrs. Johnson had been every time he'd been there.

"It hasn't changed much," Trevor told Lucy when she pulled into the drive and stopped the car.

She shifted in her seat to face him. "You remember being here?"

He smiled at the surprise on her face. "Like I told you, I'd been out here several times as a kid."

"That was a long time ago."

"It was." Trevor shrugged. "But you know how Hedy's house always felt like a home?"

She gave a slow nod.

"This house had that same vibe." Trevor chuckled. "Maybe it was because flowers were always on the table, and Emily always made cream puffs."

Lucy laughed. "She still loves making them."

"I sure loved eating them." He cocked his head as a thought struck him. "Will there be cream puffs tonight?"

"I doubt it." Lucy pushed open her car door. "But I guess anything is possible."

"I'll carry in the salad." Trevor pushed open his door, then removed the dish from the back seat. Once the dish was in his hands, he stood for a second, studying the house.

The white clapboard siding and large wraparound front porch hadn't changed. The barn in the distance, also white, appeared to have been painted in the last year. Several horses stood outside in the pen, watching them.

"I don't recall the family having horses." Trevor's gaze remained on the horses even when Lucy moved to stand beside him.

Her lips curved in a slight smile. "They were Kevin's. He loved these three. They're Icelandic horses. Their names are Dasher, Dancer and Vixen."

"They look more like ponies than horses."

"They're about fourteen hands." After casting one last look at the horses, Lucy started toward the house.

Trevor fell into step beside her.

As they passed several cars lined up in the drive, Trevor realized he hadn't asked how big—or small—this get-together was going to be.

By the time he opened his mouth to ask, he and Lucy already stood on the porch. The door immediately opened, and Sam and Stella greeted them with welcoming smiles.

Stella gave Lucy a hug before shifting her attention to Trevor. "I'm glad you could make it."

"Thanks for letting me tag along with Lucy." He nearly called himself her plus-one, but knew Lucy didn't consider this a dating situation.

"You come bearing gifts." Sam gestured to the container in Trevor's hands.

"Watergate salad. Made it myself," Trevor deadpanned.

"That's wonderful," Stella told him.

Lucy jabbed Trevor in the side with her elbow.

"Okay, to be completely factual, she made it, and I helped." Trevor smiled, thinking of last night when he'd brought pizza over to Lucy's house. They'd capped off the evening by making the salad.

"Well, I'm sure it's delicious." Stepping aside, Stella motioned them into the warmth.

Trevor glanced around. The furniture might have changed, but he couldn't be sure. When he was a kid, he hadn't paid much attention to furnishings. He remembered the cream puffs and that Emily, Sam and Kevin's mom, had kind eyes and that she and her husband, Geoff, appeared to actually like each other.

Sam and Stella appeared to be following in Sam's parents' footsteps in terms of the love thing. They shared little touches and glances as they took his and Lucy's coats, then set out the salad on a table already filled with an abundance of side dishes. Slices of turkey filled a platter in the center of the table.

"Help yourself," Sam told him. "Instead of sitting around a table, we've gone with the buffet approach this year. Grab yourself some food and mingle."

Stella gestured. "There's beer and sodas in the cooler and wine on the table over there. Like Sam said, please help yourself."

"Is there something I can do to help?" Lucy asked.

"Enjoy yourself," Stella told her.

Lucy smiled. "I can do that."

Trevor took a little of everything, amazed at the choices and the informality. He'd thought—assumed—everyone would be seated in the kitchen, since that's the way it had been when he'd had Thanksgiving at Hedy's.

Instead, everyone wandered between the kitchen and living room, where a football game—on low volume—played on the screen, eating and talking.

"I understand you knew my husband and his brother growing up." Stella sipped her glass of Pinot and offered a friendly smile.

Since he and Lucy had arrived, Sam's wife had gone out of her way to make him feel welcome.

"I did. For several years, anyway." Trevor took a sip of beer, glancing over to where Lucy was laughing with Kate.

She looked incredible, he thought. When she smiled, her entire face glowed.

When he turned back, Stella was smiling. "You moved away when you were young, but I can't remember if my husband told me where you went. Or maybe he didn't know."

"Kentucky," Trevor supplied, then received a hard slap on the back and turned.

"Hey, looks like they're inviting just about anyone to these events nowadays." Derek flashed a bright smile. "Good to see you, man."

"Now that you've got a couple weeks under your belt, tell me how it feels being back." Derek took a drink of beer, appearing genuinely interested.

"Different," Trevor said honestly. "It's the same, but not the same, if that makes sense."

"I can see how it would feel that way," Sam said, stepping into the conversation. "There's been an amazing amount of business growth, and the population continues to inch upward, which, considering how many small communities are losing population, is very encouraging."

"There's also a number of people who used to live here who've come back," Derek reminded Sam, then turned to Trevor. "Where is it you call home now?"

"Knoxville." Trevor caught Lucy gazing in his direction and smiled before refocusing on Derek and Sam. "It's a nice town."

"I'm sure it is." Sam sipped his wine, his expression turning thoughtful. "Have you ever considered leaving the warmth of the South behind and moving north?"

Trevor knew what Sam was really asking. "I've considered it.

So far, I'm enjoying being back in Holly Pointe. I told Hedy I'd stay until the end of the year. After that, we'll see."

When he'd first hit the Holly Pointe city limits, Trevor had had no idea how he'd feel. After all, he'd been gone for more years than he'd lived here. Right now, he felt like a person experiencing the community for the first time. Still, he was impressed.

"A group of us are planning to get together this coming Wednesday at six for pond hockey." Derek inclined his head. "You'd be welcome."

"I haven't skated in years."

"Then you can be on the other team." Derek chuckled at his own joke. "Seriously, skating is like riding a bike." He glanced down at Trevor's feet. "Looks like we still wear the same size. I've got an extra pair of skates I can bring you."

"What do you have an extra pair of, Derek?"

As Lucy joined the group to stand beside Trevor, everything in him relaxed.

"Trevor is going to join us at Star Lake on Wednesday." Derek's eyes took on a mischievous glow. "He hasn't skated since he left us. I told him I'd put him on your team."

"The teams are co-ed?" Trevor couldn't hide his surprise.

"Don't look so shocked, Trev," Lucy teased. "I bet I can still outskate you."

"I don't—" he began.

"I *am* the reining Reindeer Games champ." She blew on her nails and pretended to buff them on the front of her dress.

"Reindeer Games?" Sam's brows pulled together. "What is that?"

Lucy laughed. "Just something Hedy cooked up for us when we were kids."

"She'd make up these competitions to keep us occupied." Trevor grinned, thinking back to the various challenges.

"Those competitions were my favorite part of Christmas." Lucy's lips curved, and he could see she was looking back.

"Highlight of my year," Trevor agreed.

"It sounds like fun." Stella slid an arm around Sam's back and smiled at Lucy and Trevor.

"Lots of good memories," Trevor agreed, realizing that all of his best memories in Holly Pointe revolved around Lucy and Hedy.

There would be more good memories to make this year, he told himself, his gaze settling on Lucy. For all of them.

He'd make sure of it.

After eating way too much, Trevor and Lucy stayed for one game of holiday charades, then called it a night.

Though everyone hated to see them leave, when he told them he and Lucy needed to pick up his grandmother from the Candy Cane Christmas House, they understood.

The weather had turned to sleet by the time they reached town. Trevor pulled his truck as close as he could to the three-story house so that his grandmother wouldn't have to walk far. Though Christmas was six weeks away, the décor of the house and yard reminded him of the Vegas Strip at midnight.

Lighted candy canes shone their brightness on his path. What looked to be a million colored lights were wrapped about the old Victorian's turrets. White icicle lights hung from the eaves of the porch, while the railings were wrapped in greenery and bows and festooned with even more lights.

"Maybe I should put on my sunglasses," Trevor said to Lucy.

She only grinned.

As he reached the porch guarded by two goofy-looking elves, he had to smile again. Heck, everything tonight made him smile.

He hadn't been sure that he'd made the right move when he'd shown up in Holly Pointe without any notice. As soon as he'd seen his grandmother's face, though, he'd known coming had been the right decision. When she'd wrapped her arms around him, he'd nearly lost it. This was the only mother he'd ever known, and he hadn't done right by her.

He should have contacted her long ago, if only to thank her for everything she'd done for him when he'd been a kid.

The door opened, and Mary Pierson motioned him and Lucy inside. His grandmother had mentioned Mary had been very sick a year or so ago, but tonight she looked healthy to him. When he'd dropped Gran off earlier, he'd watched Mary stride across the main parlor to help one of the women with the cinnamon pumpkin candle she'd been making.

"Trevor." Mary smiled warmly at him, then shifted her gaze to Lucy. "And, Lucy, it's so good to see you."

"You brought Lucy with you." Hedy appeared in the doorway that Trevor assumed led to the kitchen. "This is a special treat."

Hedy crossed the parlor with sure, confident strides. If the knee she'd injured last spring bothered her, it didn't show. She hugged Lucy first, then Trevor. "Please tell me you didn't leave the party early to pick me up."

"We were ready to go," Lucy told her before he had the chance. "Omigod, Hedy, there was so much food, and it was all incredible."

"You'll have to tell me all about it," Hedy told Lucy, looping her arm through hers.

On the way to Hedy's home, Lucy gave her a blow-by-blow of the entire evening, including each side dish.

Seeing the closeness between the two women warmed Trevor's heart. Hedy might not have had blood relatives around, but she hadn't been without family. Her friends and Lucy had filled that gap.

Once they reached Hedy's driveway, she invited Lucy inside for a cup of tea.

Trevor assumed Lucy would say no. After all, she'd had a long day and would likely be up early tomorrow.

As she had so many times, Lucy surprised him.

"Do you have any of that Sleepytime tea?" Lucy asked.

"It's the only thing I drink in the evening." Hope filled his grandmother's eyes. "I've missed you, Lucy."

"I've missed you, too." Lucy reached forward from the back seat to squeeze Hedy's shoulder. "When you retired, I thought we'd still see each other all the time. But you got busy. I was busy—"

"Well, we're together now." Hedy gave her head a definitive shake. "And right now, the two of us and Trevor are going to enjoy a cup of Sleepytime together."

CHAPTER EIGHT

Once inside, the two women headed straight for the kitchen as if that was the place to be. Trevor followed them into the room with its pale yellow walls and white curtains with multicolored embroidered flowers along the bottom.

A vintage—okay, old—Formica-topped table edged in chrome was flanked by four chairs with red vinyl on the seats and backs.

"Have a seat, boy." Hedy gestured with one hand toward the table, then turned to Lucy. "I've got some pumpkin cookies with cream cheese frosting in the refrigerator."

"I'll get them out." Lucy turned toward the Frigidaire that Trevor swore was the same one that had been in the house when he was a kid.

Instead of sitting as instructed, Trevor grabbed some cups, plates and napkins. His heart gave a lurch when one of the cups he pulled out was a World's Best Grandma mug he'd given Hedy for Christmas the year before he'd left Holly Pointe.

He turned with the red mug with the white lettering in hand. "You are, you know."

Hedy turned from the kettle she'd set on the stove, a questioning look in her eye. He saw the instant she spotted the mug in his hand. Her expression softened. "I treasure that mug. No one but me can use it."

Lucy straightened with the container of cookies in her hands and smiled. "You may not be my grandma by blood," she told Hedy, "but in my heart, where it counts, you are."

"You two best just stop." Hedy blinked rapidly as tears filled her eyes. "All this talk is going to go straight to my head."

Trevor set the table.

Lucy took the cookies from the sealed plastic container, placed several on a pretty plate, then set the cookies in the center of the table.

The kettle began to sing. Hedy brought out the tea bags and filled the mugs with steaming water.

Once they were at the table, Hedy turned to Lucy. "I can't wait to hear what happened with Pretty. It's been the talk of Holly Pointe."

While Lucy updated Hedy, Trevor leaned back in his seat and munched on the best pumpkin cookie he'd ever eaten. A feeling of contentment settled around his shoulders as the wind howled outside.

The change in weather likely meant another storm was moving in, but in the cozy kitchen under the soft glow of the overhead fluorescent light, the rattling of the windows barely registered.

His gaze shifted to Lucy, who was giving Hedy the blow-by-blow of the emu's escape and subsequent capture, and Hedy, whose gaze was firmly fixed on Lucy.

Hedy laughed and shook her head. "I can't believe Frank Dobbs thought it was a good idea to bring an emu into the Marketplace."

Lucy grinned. "I can't believe I approved it."

"And all this was going on while there was a leak in the Baby Barn?"

"Austin and his crew had already patched the roof by the time

I arrived and saw the water on the floor." Lucy glanced at Trevor, and her smile warmed him to the core. "Trevor and I had that chapel back in shape in no time."

Hedy took a sip of tea, her gaze shifting from Lucy to Trevor. "Sounds as if you and my grandson made a good team."

"We really did," Lucy agreed in a happy tone as she took another bite of cookie.

"You two always did work well together." Hedy smiled. "Remember the time you decided to build a treehouse in the backyard?"

Until now, Trevor had forgotten all about the treehouse. "We were what, nine or ten?"

"We got those old boards from that place over on Daltry that they were demolishing." Lucy smiled at the memory, then her gaze grew thoughtful. "I don't recall where we got the hammer and nails..."

"That was courtesy of me," Hedy informed her. "I got you each a hammer and a box of nails. After that, it was all up to you."

Lucy turned to Trevor. "You drew up our plans."

"I've still got that sketch," Hedy told them.

"You do?" Trevor's eyes widened. "You kept it all this time? Why?"

"I always knew you'd be a famous artist of some sort one day." Hedy smiled. "And you are."

"You're an artist?" Lucy's voice rose in surprise.

Hedy spoke before Trevor had the chance. "He carves the most beautiful images in wood."

Lucy smiled. "I'd love to see some of your work."

"I'd love to show some of my pieces to you." Curious now, Trevor cocked his head. "What did you think I did for a living?"

"Something with computers," she said without hesitation. "You had a talent for electronics."

"I did," Trevor admitted. "But creating something from wood is, well, you could say it's my passion."

Hedy's gaze shifted from one to the other. "You two still have so much catching up to do."

Trevor nodded his agreement. "It's been a long time."

"It's been nice," Lucy said.

"What has?" Trevor asked.

"Well, so much time has gone by, but yet, we've been able to pick up where we left off with very little effort."

"Time and distance can't sever a true connection." Hedy dipped the edge of her cookie in tea, her tone matter-of-fact. "When it's there, it's there. That's what the two of you have, a true connection."

Trevor wasn't sure how to respond to that, other than to nod. He took a sip of tea and avoided looking in Lucy's direction.

When Hedy brought up the Galaxy Gals, he relaxed. For the next few minutes, he listened, drank his tea and thought about how right this felt.

Sitting at the table with Lucy and Gran, he mulled his grandmother's words. There *was* a connection between him and Lucy, one that time and distance hadn't broken.

A connection that was stronger than anything he'd felt with Anna Beth. He slanted a glance at Lucy, and their eyes locked.

Trevor smiled and realized he could be *that guy* after all. He'd just needed to find the right woman.

After she finished at the Barns on Monday, Lucy decided to grab her skates and head out to Star Lake to do a little practicing before the pond hockey game on Wednesday.

Her skating ability was strong, but when she thought about hitting the ice in two days, she realized just how long it had been since she'd skated. Several weeks ago, the ice had been deemed ready. This was earlier than usual because of the unusually cold weather in September and October.

Visitors to the area had been delighted. Anyone coming to northern Vermont at this time of year was hoping to be able to skate, snowshoe and ski.

Nearby Jay Peak provided the skiing, while Holly Pointe offered visitors everything else.

The fact that Trevor would be skating on Wednesday, too, had Lucy wanting to be at the top of her game.

The pond was nearly deserted, which was what she'd expected for a Monday evening in mid-November. Though darkness had already descended, the lights around the pond bathed the area in brightness.

Things were slow now, but once Thanksgiving was in the rearview, it would be wall-to-wall people in Holly Pointe for the rest of the season.

Lucy didn't mind. She, like the other merchants, knew the value of the tourist dollars. Besides, the visitors brought excitement and energy to the community.

Taking a seat on one of the benches surrounding the lake, Lucy exchanged her boots for skates.

"Hey, you."

Lucy blinked at the deep voice and realized that Trevor stood at the edge of the ice. "What are you doing here?" he asked.

"I could ask you the same." Lucy stepped onto the ice and began to skate, not surprised when he skated beside her.

"I haven't been on skates since leaving Holly Pointe." His lips quirked upward in a wry smile. "Since I really don't want to wipe out and embarrass myself Wednesday, I decided I'd better get out here and practice."

"Where's Hedy?"

He laughed. "Where is she every day? At the Candy Cane Christmas House helping Mary and enjoying all the commotion."

"That house is a happening place at this time of year."

"Tell me about it." Trevor negotiated the curve without any trouble. "Today, there was a group of women—and a few guys

— sampling a variety of weird Thanksgiving pies. There were some other activities planned, but I'm not sure what they were."

"Weird pies?" Lucy cocked her head.

"Okay, so maybe they didn't call them weird. That's just how I think of them."

"Give me an example."

Trevor's expression turned thoughtful. "Butternut squash pie, cranberry apple slab pie, gingersnap crumb pear pie. There are some others, but, oh, I remember another one—oatmeal rum raisin pie."

"A couple of those sound interesting."

Trevor made a face.

Lucy laughed. "I'm serious. I think I'll ask Mary for the recipe for the rum raisin one."

"I hope they don't have a piece waiting for me when I stop by to pick Hedy up later."

"Maybe, but I doubt it." Lucy had attended a few pie tastings over the years. Trevor would be lucky to find a few crumbs.

"You know who was there?"

"Who?"

"Doreen Gardner."

Lucy turned sharply and stumbled on a rough patch of ice.

She would have righted herself, but Trevor didn't give her a chance. He took her arm and steadied her. Then he looped her arm through his.

She glanced questioningly at him.

"Increased stability." He grinned. "For you. Not me. Because you were the one who almost fell."

"I didn't almost fall. I wasn't looking and—" She stopped herself when she saw his lips twitch. "That's interesting about Doreen being at the tasting. She was working the Marketplace booth earlier."

"She looked as if she was having fun." Trevor's expression

turned thoughtful. "Has her husband given you any more trouble?"

"No." Lucy expelled a breath. "But I don't think I've heard the last of him yet."

Trevor slanted a glance in her direction. "You said you booked a corporate event when the Mistletoe Ball usually is. What's the company?"

"I rented the Big Barn out to Burton Coffee Roasters. They're a Vermont-based company, and this will be their first time in Holly Pointe. It'll be a two-day event the weekend before Christmas."

"Normally, you lose money on the ball."

"We break even—"

"You get no money for the use of the Barn, so essentially you were leaving money on the table."

From a purely business perspective, he'd nailed it.

"That's true." Lucy was glad they were skating. The motion soothed her jangled nerves, and her arm around Trevor's gave her support. "I really need the revenue this month. Most people in town understand, though there are a few who refuse to see any side but their own. If Kevin were here, he'd tell me bringing the town together to celebrate Christmas should be the priority."

"Maybe." Trevor's tone remained easy. "I heard Kevin ended up being Mr. Christmas, and that's great. But from what I recall of him, he was also smart. If he knew you needed the money and why, I bet he'd be on board with your decision."

Lucy wondered if Trevor was aware of how much his assessment of Kevin's response meant to her.

"Lucy."

She turned at the sound of her name being called and smiled. "Marleigh. Hello. I haven't seen you lately."

Marleigh Hoskins, a seamstress in town, had been a high school classmate of Lucy's.

"It has been a few weeks," Marleigh agreed. She held the hand of her first-grade daughter.

"Hey, Kendra." Lucy smiled at the child. "You're lookin' good on those skates."

Kendra's answering smile showed two missing front teeth.

"We thought we'd get some skating time in."

Lucy was about to introduce her to Trevor when Marleigh continued. "Lucy, I hope you'll reconsider canceling the Mistletoe Ball. It's not only such an important tradition, I'm losing the boost in revenue the ball brings. I can't even tell you how many people come to me every year to have a dress made or altered." Marleigh glanced at her daughter. "We've always used the extra money for Christmas."

"Next year," Lucy promised. "I can't do anything about this year. I'm sorry, Marleigh."

"Have you considered having the ball on Christmas Eve or Christmas Day?" Marleigh ignored her daughter's tugging on her hand.

"That's been brought up, but I can't ask my employees to work on a day meant for family." Lucy glanced at Kendra and smiled.

"I just thought I'd ask. I know you're doing your best." Marleigh skated off before Lucy could say another word.

Lucy turned to Trevor. "I'd have introduced you, but she didn't give me the chance."

"I remember her." Trevor's gaze searched Lucy's face. "It appears not holding the ball is a big deal to a lot of people."

"It'll be an even bigger deal if the ownership of the Barns is no longer local."

"Instead of canceling entirely, is there another location that would be able to handle the crowd?"

"I brought that up, but according to event organizers, there is no other venue large enough."

"What about if the age limit was raised to twenty-one?"

Trevor pressed. "Or if they got rid of the band and went with a DJ instead?"

"Everyone was opposed to changing the age because it might discourage tourists, and it goes against tradition. Going with a DJ is a good idea, but that wouldn't be enough of a change to help with the revenue issue." A wave of sadness washed over Lucy. "If it were a different year and the financial situation were different, I might be able to find a solution."

"You're a service provider, not the event organizer. They are the ones who are supposed to problem-solve. For the people in Holly Pointe to be pressuring you--someone who has been helping them out for years by providing a venue free of charge--doesn't make sense."

CHAPTER NINE

On Wednesday, Lucy hadn't needed any help at Grace Hollow, so Trevor spent the day with Hedy. He discovered she'd set aside this Wednesday to pick up her Thanksgiving turkey. When he reminded her that Thanksgiving wasn't until next week, she'd told him that by next week, all the good birds would be gone.

The bird she got was big enough to feed an army. When Trevor had asked Hedy if Mary would be joining him, she'd told him Mary had left for New York City to spend Thanksgiving with her family there. It had made Trevor extra glad to know he'd be here to celebrate with his grandmother.

As much as he'd enjoyed his time with his grandmother, all he could think about was that he'd see Lucy later.

He glanced at the men and women in their skates, their parkas and gloves laughing and talking as if the temperature was a balmy seventy-five instead of thirty.

"We've got a new player today," Derek was saying, then lifted a hand in greeting as a man in a dark parka and hat approached. "Dustin. I didn't realize you and Krista were in town already."

"Just got in last night." Dustin, tall with an athletic build, grinned. "Rosie told me I'd find you here."

"We were just getting ready to pick teams," Derek told him. "How about you be a captain, and I'll be the other?"

"Works for me." Dustin glanced around the group. "If that's okay with y'all."

Trevor smiled at the Southern drawl. It appeared basing *Down Home with Dustin & Krista* in a Southern state had caused the Minnesota-born Dustin to change his speech patterns.

He'd probably spoken that way when Trevor had been on their show, but the accent was so common in Tennessee that Trevor hadn't noticed.

"Y'all?" Zach Adamson, Derek's partner in a construction company, smiled.

"Give me two weeks," Dustin promised. "The accent will be gone."

"I think it's cute." Lucy flashed a good-natured smile.

"Time to start picking." Derek glanced at Dustin. "Because I'm such a nice guy, you can pick first."

Dustin shot another glance around the group. "Trevor."

Trevor skated over to where Dustin had positioned himself on the ice. "Other than some practice on Monday, I haven't been on skates in years."

"You sent our ratings the week you were on the show into the stratosphere," Dustin told him. "I couldn't let you be picked last."

"Wait." Lucy frowned. "You two know each other?"

"Lucy," Derek called out, putting an end to any further discussion.

"Zach," Dustin called out.

Having Lucy on a different team crushed Trevor's hope that they could play side by side, but when he shot her a glance, and she lifted her hands, he realized she wasn't the only one disappointed.

Once the two men finished picking their teams, the fun began.

Trevor discovered that he wasn't a horrible player. Maybe not a great one, but Derek had been right about skating being like riding a bike. Thanks to Monday's practice session with Lucy, he felt comfortable on skates.

Though he could make his way across the ice without falling, what he lacked was the ability to handle the stick effectively and pass efficiently, both skills necessary in hockey.

After a rousing battle in which Trevor knew Dustin—a former NHL MVP—held back, his team still won by three goals, though Lucy ended up scoring the last goal for her team.

"Way to go, Luce," he called out.

"If this was the Reindeer Games, I'd be the winner."

"Reindeer Games?" Derek asked as he and Zach skated to a stop beside them.

"Different challenges Hedy cooked up for us when we were kids," Trevor told him.

"A competition that involved all sorts of activities."

"It's like you two had your own little world," Derek mused.

"It's like they still do," Zach said.

Trevor just laughed.

For a moment, Trevor considered hanging around to speak with Dustin. He was curious about the text Dustin had sent him saying he had something to discuss with him and hoped they'd find a time to meet while they were both in Holly Pointe.

But the tourists who'd come to watch the game surrounded the star as soon as the game ended.

Once Trevor removed his skates, he fell into step beside Lucy. "That was an amazing feint. I really thought you were going for the left side of the net."

"Thanks." Lucy smiled. "But Zach is easy to fool."

"Where are you headed now?"

"Back to Grace Hollow." Lucy's tone remained upbeat. "The Marketplace should be closing soon."

"Do you have to be there? Don't you have someone on-site who closes up?"

"Austin is working tonight. I really shouldn't have left him as it is."

"I understand. I was just hoping you'd have time for a quick dinner first."

Lucy cocked her head as if this was the first time the thought of food had entered her mind. "What are you thinking?"

"You." He pointed to her, then to himself. "Me. Wherever you want. Quick. Slow. Your call."

"Hey, you two." Dustin called out as he passed by, a couple of teenage boys and their parents following behind. "Great game."

"You were on his show," Lucy said to Trevor, as if suddenly recalling Dustin's earlier comment.

Trevor seized the opening. "Grab something to eat with me, and I'll regale you with my life as a television star."

"I'm seriously tempted," Lucy said. "But I can't. I really need to get back to the Barns and take over for Austin."

"Another time, then."

"I'd like that." When they stopped at her car, Lucy turned back to him. "Thanks for understanding."

Then she rose up on her tiptoes and brushed her lips across his cheek.

The idea had seemed like such a good one, Trevor thought, as he balanced the tray of food in one hand and used the key Lucy had given him to unlock the door to the Baby Barn. Now that he was here, he found himself having second thoughts.

Lucy was still on-site, but other than a van belonging to the cleaning crew, her car was the last one in the lot. That part at least was going according to plan.

After stopping at the Christmas House, Trevor had swung by Jingle Shells, then headed to the Barns.

Fully committed now to the plan, he strode through the area, searching for the perfect spot. He found it in the chapel area, where moonlight bathed the flowers and greenery in a golden glow.

Pulling out his phone, he texted Lucy.

In the chapel. Come whenever you're free.

He didn't want her to drop whatever she was doing and rush over, thinking this was some kind of emergency, but he knew the text would pique her curiosity. She wouldn't be able to stay away for long.

Which was good, because the food he'd brought wouldn't stay warm forever. While he waited, he made himself useful getting everything set up.

It was only a matter of minutes before footsteps echoed in the empty building.

She stepped into the doorway and just stood there, staring.

At him.

At the picnic blanket spread on the floor.

At the bottle of wine and two glasses.

"What is this?"

The delight in her voice had everything in him relaxing.

"I thought you might be hungry, but knew you didn't have time to go out, so I brought the restaurant to you." Trevor took a seat on the blanket and patted the spot next to him. "Please. Join me."

With an effortless grace that was as much a part of her as that sunny smile, Lucy sat beside him.

He lifted the bottle. "Wine?"

She took one of the glasses and held it out. "I'd love some."

He poured her a healthy portion of the red, then splashed some into the other glass for himself before setting the bottle aside.

Lucy took a sip of wine. "This is good."

"I aim to please." He grinned. "Wait until you see what I

cooked up. Well, I didn't actually make this, but I did choose what to get."

"What exactly did you get?" Lucy gazed at him over the rim of her wineglass. "Whatever it is, it smells wonderful."

"It's a sampler platter from Jingle Shells," he told her, taking the lid off the container. "There's a little bit of everything in here. We have Linguine with Santa Claws, which is crab, Frosty the Sno-Manicotti, Fa-La-La-Lasagna and Fettuccini Alfred-Ho-Ho-Ho and—"

"Just the names make me smile." Lucy pointed to another container. "What's in that?"

"That's for later." Trevor handed her a plate. "Bon appétit."

She hesitated. "How are we going to divide this? I assume you haven't eaten."

"I'll eat whatever you don't want."

She laughed. "I want it all, just not this much. What if we split each dish in half? Does that work?"

Her happiness wrapped around him like a favorite shirt. "Works for me."

They'd eaten in comfortable silence for several minutes when Lucy slanted a glance in Trevor's direction. "We've talked about a lot of things, but other than a few bits and pieces, you haven't told me much about your life once you left Holly Pointe."

"What is it you want to know?"

"Everything." She sipped her wine and studied him over the rim of the glass.

While Trevor didn't usually talk much about that time in his life, he liked that she was interested enough to ask.

"Okay. You and I both know that when my mother showed up to take me with her and Chad to Kentucky, I didn't want to go. When it appeared to be a done deal, I tried to be positive. I hoped maybe we could be a family. That maybe Chad could be the father I never had."

"Let me guess." Lucy cocked her head and tapped a finger against her lips. "That didn't happen."

"Bingo." Trevor gave a humorless laugh. "It quickly became apparent that my mother still had no interest in me. Which meant that although I had a roof over my head and they bought me clothes, I was on my own."

"What about Chad?"

"Ignored me."

"I'm so sorry, Trevor." Lucy set down her glass, and sympathy shimmered in her blue eyes. "You were all alone."

"I was, until I became acquainted with Ray." Trevor recalled the first day he'd met the retired factory worker. "Ray Geller lived down the street in a house that he and his wife had owned for forty-two years. He was always working out in his yard. His dog, a blonde cocker named Sugar, was always right by his side. One day, I asked if I could pet Sugar, and Ray and I got to talking."

"You said he was retired? So he was older?"

"He had gray hair. He seemed old to me, but then, when you're twelve, all adults seem old."

Lucy chuckled. "True."

"Ray was extremely talented. He was also patient and kind." Trevor expelled a breath. "He never asked why I was out so late at night or why I was often hungry when I stopped over. I think he knew my home life was less than stellar and wasn't going to add to my burden by acting like a cop and questioning me."

"Ray became your surrogate grandfather."

Though Trevor had never thought of the older gentleman in those terms, Lucy's assessment fit. He nodded. "I guess he was."

"You said he was talented." As Lucy leaned forward to pour herself more wine, the lights overhead bathed her face in a soft golden glow. Even though she was looking at the bottle, Trevor could feel that her attention was on him. But then, no matter where they were, Lucy had always made him feel like the most important person in the room. "What was his talent?"

"Carving. Specifically carving figures into wood. A discarded piece of driftwood, a stump, a log, just about anything." Trevor remembered every one of Ray's creations, and they were all amazing. "I think Ray saw me as a boy on the edge. I mean, I was a good kid at heart, but I was struggling to find my place. I felt as if I didn't belong anywhere. Gangs in big cities are filled with kids like me, kids looking for a family and a place to belong. Ray and Marcia gave that to me."

"They took you in."

It was as if she knew the combination of the warmth, the quiet and a sympathetic ear encouraged confidences. If that was what she thought, she was on target.

Trevor relaxed back on his elbows. "I spent most of the time when I wasn't in school at his house."

"Did your mother approve?"

"I think she was just glad I wasn't around."

"So Ray was a good person?" The worry in Lucy's voice had him reaching over to squeeze her hand. He'd forgotten how much she liked happy endings.

"Ray was—is—one of the most honest and ethical men I've ever met."

Lucy slipped her hand from his, but not before letting it rest in his for a full ten seconds. "I'm glad."

"He paid attention to my grades and taught me not only to carve, but what it meant to be a man."

"You've done well for yourself."

He heard the question in the comment.

"I have. Ray encouraged me, bolstered my confidence, encouraged me to take risks with my art. I was already showing promise and had some showings when I was in high school." Trevor's lips curved as he recalled his argument, er, conversation, with Ray when high school graduation had loomed. "I wanted to do art full time. Ray insisted I take business classes at the community college. I didn't see the point. He wouldn't budge."

"Did you take the classes?"

"I respected his opinion too much to ignore it." Trevor shifted his gaze out the window. "He also hooked me up with a counselor. He said the baggage I was carrying around would drag me under if I didn't find a way to cut it loose. He said something to the effect that we all carry around these backpacks filled with emotional baggage. We think we're doing just fine until the backpack becomes too full, and all the stuff falls out."

They sat in silence for several seconds.

Trevor didn't know what to think when Lucy rested her head against his shoulder. He only knew he felt himself steady as he inhaled the vanilla scent that was uniquely her.

"Where is Ray now?"

"He and Marcia are still in Lexington. They're doing great. I swear those two are still as happy as the day they walked down the aisle." Trevor smiled, remembering the time he'd caught them kissing in the kitchen.

"What did they think of Anna Beth?"

Lucy's question had Trevor's smile faltering.

"They thought she was a good person." Trevor fought to be honest. "Which she is. But—"

Lucy offered an encouraging smile.

"Ray told me he didn't see that spark between us." Trevor chuckled. "I told him not everyone can have what he and Marcia have. He told me all I needed was the right person."

"A wise man." Lucy's gaze searched his face. "I'd like to meet him sometime."

"I think Ray and Marcia would enjoy a trip to Holly Pointe. They've got a nice family, too, kids, grandkids—they all made me feel like part of their family."

"Kevin's family did that, too."

"Do you still get together with them?"

"Sometimes. Not as much as before."

"It's like that with Ray and his family." Trevor knew he'd always be welcome in Ray's home. "Marcia is this fabulous cook and—" He broke off. "I almost forgot." He reached for the container that he'd set off to the side and handed it to Lucy. "This is for you."

"What is it?"

"Open it and find out."

Lifting the top open, Lucy gazed down, then back up at Trevor. "Is this what I think it is?"

"A slice of oatmeal rum raisin pie." Trevor watched the smile spread over her lips. "Just for you."

"Just for us." Her gaze met his. "This is one of the nicest things anyone has ever done for me."

"Maybe you should take a bite first," he told her. "See if it tastes good or not."

"Okay." Lucy picked up the plastic fork, forked off a bite, then brought the piece to her lips.

Trevor watched her full red lips close over the fork, and an ache of longing to have that mouth on his rose up inside him.

Lucy closed her eyes, and her expression turned dreamy. Then she opened her eyes and smiled.

"How is it?"

"Amazingly good." Using the same fork, she scooped up another bite and held it out to him. "You try."

He kept his eyes on her as he leaned forward and closed his mouth over the fork.

"What do you think?"

Trevor couldn't hide his surprise. "It tastes like an oatmeal cookie crossed with pecan pie."

"I know." Lucy grinned. "I love it."

Trevor found himself wishing they could sit here together forever like this, talking and laughing in the quiet.

The buzz of his phone had him frowning. He ignored it.

"You should check," Lucy urged. "It could be Hedy."

"You're right." Trevor pulled out the phone and quickly read the message. "It's from Dustin. He wants to talk."

"What about?"

"I'm not sure."

"How did you end up on their show?"

"They saw my work at a showing in Nashville, and their representative contacted me. It went well. Lots of sales and good publicity."

Dustin and Krista had leveraged their fame as a former NHL superstar and supermodel to build a show that would showcase independent artists of all persuasions.

"Will you show me your art sometime?"

"I'd be happy to."

Lucy heaved a sigh. "I suppose I should call it a night."

"You've had a long day."

Even after the words were spoken, they sat for several more seconds as if both realized that once they stood up, this closeness, or whatever it was they were building, could vanish.

When she curved her fingers around his wrist, he smiled and shot her a questioning glance.

"Thank you for the food and for sharing your story with me." Then she leaned over and kissed him on the mouth.

By the time his lips caught up to his brain, she'd stood and was packing up the remnants of their impromptu picnic, leaving him no choice but to help her put an end to their wonderful evening.

CHAPTER TEN

Thanksgiving ended up being a quiet affair for Trevor. Hedy had invited Lucy to join them, but Kevin's parents were in town, and she'd already promised to spend the holiday at the farm with them.

Trevor helped out Friday at the Marketplace while Lucy was occupied by events being held in the Baby Barn.

"Thanks for your help, man." Austin took off his ball cap and wiped the sweat from his forehead as they entered the break room to take fifteen. "With Joseph out sick, we really needed an extra man."

"I've never seen so many people in here." Though the customers he'd seen all appeared to be in high spirits, Trevor knew there wasn't anything that would cause him to get out in this crowd.

"Saleswise, this is the biggest day for the vendors," Austin informed him, pulling a soda from the machine and giving it to Trevor before getting one for himself.

"I can believe it." Trevor took a long sip and let the cool, sweet taste slide down his throat. "I wonder how Lucy is coming in the Baby Barns. Maybe I should—"

"I just spoke with her not fifteen minutes ago." Austin dropped into one of the chairs. "Everything there is under control."

"That's good." Personally, Trevor had hoped Lucy would need extra help. He was willing and eager to take on that task.

"I saw Geoff and Emily stopped by."

"Here? They were in the Marketplace?"

"This morning," Austin confirmed. "They were making the rounds with Stella and Sam."

"Do they come back to Holly Pointe often?"

"It varies depending on what's going on in New York." Austin eyed him. "You know he's a playwright, and she's a Broadway producer."

"I did know that. When I lived here as a kid, I was friends with Kevin and Sam."

"I knew you'd lived here before." Austin eyed him curiously. "I didn't realize you were friends with Kevin. He passed away before I moved here, but based on what everyone says, he was a great guy."

"He was a boy when I knew him." Trevor smiled. "He had this huge imagination. It wouldn't have surprised me if he'd ended up a playwright like his dad."

Austin brought the can of cola to his lips and studied Trevor. Then he lowered it without drinking. "You know he and Lucy were involved."

"I know they were engaged."

"I never knew them as a couple. I came on board shortly after he passed away. Lucy was a wreck, but she kept working."

Trevor thought of Lucy soldiering on alone. Paula wouldn't have been a comfort to her daughter. The woman just didn't have it in her.

If he'd been here, perhaps…

Trevor stopped the thought before it could fully form.

"I can't imagine how hard that must have been for her."

Austin's gaze turned assessing. "You two have been spending time together."

"We have." Trevor flashed a smile. "But not today."

Today, Lucy had been everywhere but near him. He knew it wasn't deliberate, but he missed having her close. He hadn't even had a chance to ask how her Thanksgiving had gone.

Was she avoiding him? Was she regretting kissing him last week?

That night as he was leaving, he couldn't resist swinging by the Baby Barn. But when he saw Lucy was busy speaking with a customer, he kept walking.

Though it wasn't all that late when Lucy arrived home, she felt as if she'd worked a double shift. Tomorrow the tree would be lit in the town square. Kenny as Santa Claus would be hearing Christmas wishes, and all the businesses in the downtown area would be open.

The Marketplace would also be open, but only until six. Closing early allowed the vendors to attend the tree lighting with their friends and family.

But right now, she wouldn't worry about tomorrow. Her day was over, and she was ready to relax. She kicked off her shoes, poured herself a glass of wine and opened the blinds on her front window.

The colored Christmas lights around the window winked on and off. Lucy sat in the overstuffed chair and settled in to watch the snow fall. After a long day, she didn't want the noise of the television. Fatigue had her yawning, but it was too early to call it a night. If she went to bed now, she wouldn't be able to sleep anyway. Not with the way her mind was whirling.

All day long, she'd done her best to avoid thinking about that moment when she'd kissed Trevor. Not a brush of her lips across his cheek, but a real kiss.

Though she hadn't lingered, the heat that had flared when her mouth had met his had her wanting to linger. Had her wanting to wrap her arms around his neck and feel the heat from his body against hers.

Why had she done that? They'd had a lovely evening, and the picnic dinner had been sweet and thoughtful. She'd enjoyed their conversation, but then again, they'd done a lot of talking this past month, and she hadn't kissed him before.

What did this mean? What must he be thinking?

A wave of guilt washed over Lucy as she glanced around the home she'd once shared with Kevin. The lights around the window were ones they'd picked out for their first Christmas in the house.

So many memories of her and Kevin together had been forged within these four walls. So many plans for the future.

Now, here she was thinking of how good it had felt to kiss another man.

The buzzing of her phone had her jumping.

She glanced around, trying to recall where she'd left it. Spotting it, she pushed to her feet and padded in her stockinged feet to the side table by the front door.

She saw that it was a text from Mary.

I'm hoping you are still planning to come by and help me decorate my tree.

Lucy groaned aloud. She'd forgotten all about her promise to the older woman. Her fingers flew across the keyboard.

On my way.

Lucy checked her emails, found one from Austin and answered it immediately. There was also a text from her mother that she'd somehow missed seeing. She would reply to it tomorrow.

The last thing she wanted was to get her mom in the habit of expecting an instant reply.

Lucy glanced at her leggings and sweater and decided she looked good enough to decorate a tree.

On her way out the door, it struck her that maybe getting out and doing something fun was just what she needed to take her mind off Trevor.

Lucy expected to start decorating as soon as she crossed the threshold of the Candy Cane Christmas House. She realized that wasn't likely when she stepped inside and found Trevor and Hedy there.

Mary smiled broadly, gesturing with one hand. "I found helpers."

"I can see that." Lucy smiled at Hedy and Trevor before returning her attention to Mary. "How are Faith and Graham? And the girls? I bet they're getting big."

"You'd hardly recognize them." Mary shook her head, the smile wide on her lips. "It was wonderful being able to spend Thanksgiving with them."

Faith was one of Lucy's closest friends. She'd been happy when she had met and married Graham, but sad to see Faith leave Holly Pointe. The twins had been happy to have Faith as a mother after losing their own at a young age.

"I hope you told Faith how much we all miss her."

"I did," Mary assured her. "She misses you as well and told me to give you a big hug from her."

Hedy moved to Lucy then and enfolded her in an embrace so warm it brought tears to Lucy's eyes. "It's so good to see you. Trevor told me you had a busy day."

Lucy's lips lifted in a rueful smile. "The day after Thanksgiving is always hectic."

"I remember." Hedy shook her head and took a sip of her drink. "I don't miss that craziness."

Lucy slanted a glance at Trevor. "Austin told me you were a huge help today."

Hedy's brows pulled together in confusion. "Why did Austin need to tell you? Didn't Trevor help you?"

"Lucy was busy with things in the Baby Barn," Trevor told his grandmother. "Austin needed help in the Marketplace."

"Oh, that makes sense." Hedy looped her arm through Lucy's. "How was your Thanksgiving?"

Lucy caught sight of Trevor's curious look. Had he thought about her yesterday, the same way she'd thought of him?

"It was nice." Lucy saw no reason to say that she'd decided this would be the last holiday she'd spend with Kevin's family. While Geoff and Emily were wonderful and she adored Sam and Stella, she was a reminder of all they'd lost. Focus on the food, she told herself. "They had turkey and ham and too many sides to count. It was so yummy that I ate way too much. Which is probably why I skipped lunch and dinner today."

"Trevor told us the same." Hedy shook her head. "He was just about to get the leftover appetizers out when you drove up."

"It's not fun to forage for food alone." Trevor shot her an enticing smile. "Join me?"

Lucy laughed. "I never can resist an offer to forage."

Minutes later, as Lucy eased the bacon-wrapped water chestnut off the toothpick and into her mouth, she emitted a little groan.

Beside her, Trevor smiled. "I knew I should have gone for that one instead of the tortilla roll-up."

"But yours was stacked into that cute little Christmas tree shape."

"That may be true, but did it contain bacon?"

His question, coupled with a pained look, had her laughing. "Point taken."

There had been surprisingly few appetizers left from what Lucy had learned was a small gathering of Mary's friends earlier this evening.

At Mary's insistence, she and Trevor polished off what remained, along with a glass of wine and, for dessert, a couple of sugar cookies.

"Your grandmother looks so Zen." Lucy kept her tone low, knowing that the two women were just in the other room sorting through Christmas tree decorations.

"Retirement has been good for her. Though I do believe it would drive her crazy to be at home all the time. She loves being active and around people."

"That's why she was such a fabulous assistant." Lucy toyed with the stem of her wineglass. "And why I miss her so much."

"It makes her feel good to know I'm helping you," Trevor told her. "She loves you, Lucy. She really does."

"I love her, too." Which was why Lucy hadn't simply refused Trevor's offer of help. Her decision didn't have anything to do with, well, wanting Trevor around.

Even though, she thought, slanting a glance in his direction as he picked up the last appetizer on his plate, her childhood friend had definitely grown into one fine-looking man. And while she'd had only a little taste—an appetizer, really—his lips had been like the bacon-wrapped water chestnut… She found herself wanting more.

She wasn't sure why she'd kissed him. An impulse, she told herself. Not a big deal.

Trevor didn't appear to think it was a big deal. After all, he hadn't pulled her to him, or even really kissed her back, though his mouth had begun to move under hers when she'd moved back and headed inside.

No. Big. Deal.

Lucy finished off the last of her wine. "Ready to start trimming the tree?"

SNOW PLACE LIKE HOLLY POINTE | 99

Trevor looked at her with a quizzical expression. "I think that's green frosting on your lips."

Before she realized what he meant to do, he leaned forward and brushed her bottom lip with his thumb. "Yep. Frosting."

Trevor was so close, all she would need to do was lean forward a couple of inches, and…

He beat her to it. His mouth closed over hers.

Without giving herself time to overanalyze, Lucy did what she'd wanted to do all day. She wrapped her arms around his neck and fell into the kiss, the heat of his body wrapping around her like a lover's caress.

"We were wondering if you two…" Mary's voice trailed off.

Lucy dropped her arms immediately and would have stepped out of the embrace, but Trevor kept an arm around her waist, an anchor in a world of suddenly shifting sand.

Mary remained in the doorway, her gaze shifting from Trevor, who only smiled, to Lucy, who could feel the heat sting her cheeks and knew, just knew, they had to be bright pink.

"We finished our appetizers and had a couple cookies for dessert," Trevor explained.

"They were really good," Lucy added.

Mary smiled. "You can't beat a good dessert."

CHAPTER ELEVEN

When Trevor and Lucy entered the main parlor, a man who Trevor recognized as Hedy's mail carrier, Mr. Finch, and a woman he assumed was the guy's wife were playing a Christmas duet on the piano.

Trevor hadn't heard the doorbell. Had the couple just walked in and headed straight for the piano? In this town, in this particular house, it wouldn't surprise him.

He considered speaking to the two, but they appeared focused on their music, so he turned to Mary and Hedy.

"Finished with dessert?" Hedy asked.

Innocent question? Trevor wasn't sure. He smiled and resisted the urge to glance at Lucy. "For now."

"The cookies were wonderful," Lucy added.

"My mother's recipe," Mary told them. "She always said that a sugar cookie shouldn't need icing and decorations to be enjoyed. I have to admit the icing and the decorations are my favorite part."

"Well, we enjoyed them," Trevor said, smiling at Lucy.

Mary and Hedy exchanged a glance, then Mary gestured to a

large fir sitting in a corner with boxes of ornaments nearby. "I can't tell you how much your help means to me, Lucy."

"It'll be fun. I haven't decorated a tree in forever." Lucy started to say more, then stopped herself.

Trevor wondered if she'd trimmed a tree since Kevin had passed, or was she simply referring to the past few years?

"I can help." Trevor glanced at Lucy.

Lucy smiled at him. "I won't say no."

Mary clasped her hands together. "Thank you both."

"Seeing you two decorate a tree together will take me back." Hedy turned to Mary. "They used to decorate my tree every year."

"I've got an idea." Mary brightened. "Why don't you and I sit and enjoy a glass of mulled wine, along with this wonderful Christmas music, while we watch the tree turn bright and sparkly?"

"A splendid idea." Hedy shifted her gaze from Trevor to Lucy. "Let's get to it."

Trevor quickly discovered that he and Lucy worked together like a well-oiled machine. They started with the lights.

"There's a proper order to decorating a tree," Lucy informed him when he reached for some bulbs.

"We never had an order when we decorated before," Trevor protested.

"We were ten years old." Lucy chuckled and began untangling the strands of lights. "If you don't remember how those trees looked, I do."

"I thought they looked fine." Maybe time had screwed with his memories, but over the years, whenever Trevor had thought about those trees in Hedy's living room, he'd remembered the beauty.

He remembered how Hedy had encouraged him and Lucy to hang the ornaments they'd made in school and for craft projects on the tree. There had been a hodgepodge of love on every branch.

"We had lovely trees," Hedy agreed, then her voice softened. "I think Lucy is wanting this one to be extra special and maybe a little more traditional since it's in the Candy Cane Christmas House."

"That makes sense." He turned to Lucy. "You're the expert. Tell me what to do next."

"We'll start at the base and work our way up." Lucy handed him a strand of colored incandescent lights. "I'll help you wrap. We need to go from the trunk and work our way out to the tip of each branch."

Getting the lights arranged according to Lucy's specifications took time, but with the fire in the hearth adding a golden glow to the room and the piano music filling the air, placing the lights could have taken all night, and Trevor would have been happy.

Once the lights were placed, they moved to the garland, which, according to Lucy, started at the top. There were a variety of garlands ranging from thin beaded garlands to thicker foil garlands.

Trevor took a step back and studied the tree. "Even without the ornaments, this looks amazing."

"Great job, you two," the postal carrier called from the piano, his fingers still flying over the keys.

"Are you sure you and Shirley wouldn't like to take a break and enjoy some mulled wine?" Mary asked. "We have plenty."

"We appreciate the offer," Shirley Finch responded, "but practicing on your lovely piano in this wonderful house is a treat for us."

"Well, I love listening to you and your husband." Mary clasped her hands and brought them to her chest. "You're welcome here anytime."

"The Finches play a variety of Christmas melodies in the

courthouse during the gingerbread house judging," Lucy told Trevor. "It really adds to the holiday ambience."

"You know everything about everyone." Trevor reached for a shiny red ball.

"Not as much as I used to." Lucy spoke almost wistfully.

They spent the next few minutes working with a variety of sizes of red ornaments, placing the larger ones at the bottom and the smaller ones at the top.

"You've got a lot of specialty ornaments here." Lucy turned to Mary. "I'm sure some have special significance. I probably should have asked you earlier which ones you'd like on the tree."

Setting down her cup of mulled wine, Mary got up and came over to peruse the ornaments carefully displayed in their own box. She picked out several, then gave Lucy and Trevor each a hug before returning to her seat.

For several seconds, Lucy stood back and studied the tree, then, placing the ladder close, she climbed up. "I need the bulb shaped like an ice cream cone."

The vintage chandelier bathed her face and in the light her hair looked like spun gold. She reminded him of a goddess on that ladder, the perfect woman.

"Hand me the bulb shaped like an ice cream cone," she repeated. This time, her voice held an authoritative edge, one she likely used with employees who weren't paying attention.

He didn't mind. Bending over, Trevor scooped up the ornament and handed it to her. "Sorry. I guess my mind wandered or something."

Behind him, he thought he heard his grandmother snort. He whirled, concerned she might be choking. "Are you okay, Gran?"

"I was drinking too fast." Hedy lifted her cup, and he swore there was a twinkle in her eyes. "This wine is marvelous."

Trevor smiled and refocused on Lucy.

She might appear rock-steady on the ladder, but accidents

happened all the time, and he wanted to be there to catch her if she slipped.

"What one next?" he asked.

"The red glass one that looks like a pinecone dusted with snow."

He grabbed the ornament, his fingers brushing against her hand when he passed it to her. An electrical current traveled up his arm.

Lucy felt it, too. Trevor could see it when their eyes met and locked.

Then she turned back to the tree.

Had he decorated a tree since he'd left Holly Pointe? Trevor didn't think he had. There had always been a tree at Ray's house, but it had always been decorated by the time he'd seen it. His mother hadn't been into such things.

Anna Beth's parents had their trees professionally decorated. When he'd suggested once to Anna Beth that they get their own tree and decorate it, she'd looked at him as if he'd lost his mind.

So yes, this was the first time.

How odd, he thought, that the last time he'd done this had been with Lucy. Now, the two of them were together, doing it again.

When it came time to put the star at the top of the tree, Lucy paused, then glanced down at Mary. "Would you like to do the honors?"

Trevor saw then what Lucy had seen. Mary wanted to put the star on the tree, but was worrying it was beyond her.

Nothing is beyond you, Trevor remembered Ray saying. *You just have to believe.*

"Lucy and I can help steady you on the ladder." Trevor didn't push, but he met Mary's gaze firmly. He wanted Mary to know that it was possible.

"Trevor won't let you fall," Hedy told her friend. "You can put your faith in him."

A warmth spread through Trevor at his grandmother's words.

Mary's gaze shifted between him and Lucy. "I'd like that."

The piano exploded into a duet of "Have Yourself a Merry Little Christmas" while Mary carefully climbed the tall stepladder.

Lucy stood off to the side, stabilizing the ladder, while Trevor climbed up behind Mary. If she slipped, he'd be right there to catch her.

When Mary reached the point where she could put on the star, Lucy handed it to Trevor, who passed it up the ladder.

Mary placed the star at the top, and her smile shone as bright as the glittery silver star.

Hedy clasped her hands. "What a lovely, lovely tree."

Mary climbed slowly down, and when her feet hit the hardwood, Trevor put his hands on her waist until he felt her steady, then released her.

He wasn't sure what to think when she kissed his cheek. "You're a wonderful young man. I'm glad you're finally back where you belong."

Before Trevor could respond, Mary turned to Lucy and wrapped her arms around her. "You, my dear, are a gem. An absolute gem."

Lucy squeezed Mary tight. "I feel the same about you."

"If you ladies are done with your lovefest," Mr. Finch called from across the room, "the wife and I would like for you to step over here and sing along to a few tunes."

By now, it was getting late, and his grandmother was visibly fading. Yet, Trevor saw the hope in her eyes when she glanced in his direction.

He smiled. "Sounds like fun."

They were soon all gathered around the piano, with Lucy on one side of him and his grandmother on the other. When their voices blended together for familiar carols, Trevor realized that Mary had been right.

Here with Lucy and Hedy, he was finally right where he belonged.

~

While Mary and Hedy bid good night to the Finches, Lucy and Trevor took the boxes of Christmas tree decorations they hadn't used down to the basement of the old house. For the first time since they'd kissed in the kitchen, Lucy was alone with Trevor.

She took her time, adjusting the boxes on the wooden shelves, though there was really no need for them to be perfectly lined up.

"What are you doing tomorrow?"

Lucy turned and found Trevor close. Close enough that she caught a whiff of his cologne. Close enough that she could see the golden flecks in his eyes. "To-tomorrow?"

"Tomorrow." He smiled. "Saturday."

"What is it I do every day?" Her lips lifted in a rueful smile. "I'll be working at Grace Hollow. Why?"

"Do you need help?"

"Honestly, no. We have a full crew on tomorrow, so I've got everything covered."

"Okay, well, what are you doing tomorrow night?"

"Why?"

"I'd like you to go to the tree lighting with me."

"I'm sorry about kissing you, Trevor." Lucy shifted from foot to foot.

"Ah, I think I was the one who kissed you last." A tiny smile lifted his lips. "Before that was when you kissed me."

"Well, I am sorry."

"Why? I liked it and hope it will happen again. And what does you kissing me or me kissing you have to do with going with me to the tree lighting?"

"I'm just not ready."

"For?"

"For any of this." She waved a distracted hand. Maybe she should have left it at that, but from his puzzled expression, he needed more. Heck, he deserved more. "I know everyone thinks I should be ready because Kevin has been gone for so long, but I'm not."

Trevor offered an encouraging smile.

Lucy's voice rose, and the words tumbled out. "Plus, I'm busy with work, and there's all this financial stuff I need to sort out. And you just got into town after being gone for so long. You should be focused on Hedy, not—"

Trevor's hand on her shoulder stopped her midramble. "First, I am with Hedy. We both are. In case you've forgotten, she's right upstairs." His gaze searched hers, and his tone gentled even more. "I understand that work keeps you busy, and I hope you know I am ready to help in any way I can."

She nodded. "I appreciate everything you've done."

"As far as you not being ready to date, that's okay. You don't have to explain, not to me or to anyone. I don't want to pressure you, Luce. You don't need any more pressure. But I do want to spend time with you. I hope that can happen. I may have been gone for a long time, but I'm back and right here with you now."

"Okay." Lucy licked her lips. "If you'd be okay going to the tree lighting just as friends, that would work. Can it be that? Just a friendly outing?"

Trevor met her gaze and smiled. "It can be anything you want it to be."

CHAPTER TWELVE

Lucy had told Trevor she'd meet him at the tree lighting the next night. A dairy-agricultural cooperative out of Montpelier was having its annual Christmas party at the Barns. Before she left, Lucy made sure everything was going off without a hitch.

She'd designated Kinsley, a staff member with great potential, as the on-site contact person. In that role, Kins was overseeing the event. She would make sure the customer's needs were met and that all of Lucy's staff did their jobs. Which meant, unless Lucy heard from Kins, she would be able to relax and enjoy the tree lighting.

Lucy dressed warmly for the evening's event in flannel-lined jeans and a shirt under her sweater. Though her parka was arctic-rated, the temperature tonight was in the single digits with the wind making it feel even colder.

Still, the coat was one of her favorites, a bright blue that Stella had once told her made her eyes look like the sky. Lucy curled her hair and let it tumble around her shoulders in loose waves. Makeup and bright red lips had Lucy feeling festive.

What if this were a date? Would that be so horrible? For so many years, the word *date* had terrified her whenever anyone had suggested she should get back out there. It made her feel pressured and watched.

But nothing about Trevor made her feel that way. Even after all this time apart, she felt at ease with him. So, if this were a date, then maybe she was more ready than she realized.

She made her way toward the spot where they'd agreed to meet, remembering how Trevor had said that she could call it whatever she wanted. Did *he* consider it a date?

"Lucy."

When she turned and saw him wheeling his grandmother through the onlookers toward her, she had her answer.

Not a date.

Disappointment surged, but Lucy reminded herself that she'd set herself up for this. She'd told Trevor no dates and that he should spend time with Hedy, which was what he was doing tonight.

Not only was Hedy dressed warmly, she had a thick woolen blanket across her legs.

"I'm so glad you came." Lucy leaned over and gave Hedy a hug. "But what's with the wheelchair?"

"My grandson decided that, because of the number of people expected tonight, I should ride rather than walk. I swear he's more concerned about my knee than I am." But Hedy cast Trevor a loving glance as she said the words.

"I told Gran I was meeting you down here—" Trevor began.

"I hope I'm not interrupting anything—" A worried look filled Hedy's eyes as they spoke over each other.

"Are you kidding?" Lucy crouched down in front of Hedy. "I am always happy to have you around. I'm just sorry I didn't think of asking you first."

Relief crossed Trevor's face.

She couldn't believe he'd think for one minute that bringing Hedy might be a problem.

"Have you heard who's tossing the switch tonight?" Trevor

asked. "I know it's supposed to be a secret, but you know everything that goes on in this town."

Lucy did know. Sam had told Stella, who'd told Lucy. "It's supposed to be a surprise."

It had been a surprise to her, but it was a well-deserved honor.

Stella, who handled the town's marketing efforts, stepped to the microphone in front of the massive fir.

"This year, it is my distinct pleasure to introduce Rose Kelly to you. Those of you who live in Holly Pointe know Rose as a woman who has given so much to our community, one you can always call on if there's a job that needs doing. Visitors know Rose as the force behind Rosie's Diner, where everyone who walks through the door is treated like family."

Applause and whistles sounded from the crowd.

"Well, we have another job for Rose tonight—throwing the switch and lighting up this glorious tree."

More cheers from the crowd.

"Before I start the clock, I want to remind you that we'll be singing three very familiar Christmas carols once the tree is lit. If you don't know the words, they'll be displayed on our countdown board." Stella gestured with one hand toward the large electronic display that had been brought in for tonight's event. "The shops are all open late tonight, and Santa Claus will be in the courthouse to hear everyone's Christmas wishes."

Sometimes the person throwing the switch addressed the crowd before lighting the tree. It didn't surprise Lucy that Rose simply signaled Stella to start the sixty-second countdown.

Rose was a no-nonsense woman who liked to get the job— whatever job it was—done with a minimum of fanfare.

"Sixty, fifty-nine, fifty-eight..." Stella began the countdown. Those surrounding the tree quickly joined in, winding the count down to, "Three, two, one."

Rose tossed the switch, and what looked to Lucy's eyes like a zillion colors flooded the night with brilliant light.

Cheers broke out.

When those died down, the school band launched into "Silent Night," one of the three favorites they would play this evening.

Lucy knelt next to Hedy and put her arm around the older woman's shoulders so they could sway arm in arm, as they had all those years ago when Lucy had been a child, and Hedy would bring her and Trevor down to the square for the lighting.

Hedy closed her eyes as they swayed, her voice strong and sure as it blended with the hundreds of other voices.

Lucy looked up and found Trevor staring—not at his grandmother or at the gorgeous tree, but at her.

The look in his eyes stole her breath and had her smiling back.

When the third carol ended, Lucy rose, now holding Hedy's hand. "I'd love to treat you both to some cocoa."

Lucy had passed many stands selling hot drinks on her way to the meeting spot she and Trevor had picked.

"Thank you, Lucy, that's very sweet of you to offer, but I think I'm ready to head home," Hedy said.

"So soon?" Lucy's voice rose.

"I came specifically for the tree lighting and carols." Hedy offered a warm smile. "The rest of the evening is for young people."

"Sure, Gran, whatever you want." Trevor shifted his gaze to Lucy. "Ride along?"

"I'd like that."

Conversation came easy on the short drive to Hedy's bungalow. Though Lucy offered to help, Trevor told her he had it under control when he got out to help Hedy negotiate the steps that held a light dusting of snow.

Trevor soon returned to the waiting truck and its warm seats, the heat blasting. "She's all settled. Now you and I, Ms.

Cummings, are off to embrace the Christmas spirit." Trevor put the vehicle in reverse, then stopped. "Tell me where you want to go. Tonight, this pickup is your magic sleigh."

Lucy laughed. Even as a boy, Trevor had possessed a knack for pulling her out of her doldrums. "This may sound a bit silly."

He flashed a grin. "I say the sillier the better."

"We could go back to the madness that is downtown tonight, but there's something I want to do that I always promise myself I'm going to do, but I never take the time."

"Spit it out, Luce."

"I'd love to drive around and look at lights from the comfort of your truck." Once the request was out, Lucy realized just how lame it sounded. She waved her hand in the air and gave a nervous-sounding laugh. "Forget it. That's something my mom might want to do—well, might want to do if she was a different person."

Trevor grabbed the hand that fluttered in the air and kissed her knuckles, keeping his gaze firmly fixed on hers. "I think it sounds like a stellar plan."

∾

Lucy mentioned that Busy Bean had recently added a freestanding coffee and pastry drive-through. The satellite site was intended to capture the business of those who liked the convenience of ordering while remaining in their vehicles.

The fact that she'd brought up the drive-through told Trevor all he needed to know. He got a plain hot cocoa, while Lucy opted for a Santa Claus Mocha. When she mentioned the Busy Bean was now serving old-fashioned lace cookies, he added a couple to their order.

"I have to admit," Lucy dipped the edge of her cookie into the mocha, "the caramel taste goes really, really well with this mocha."

"It was a good choice." Trevor popped the last of his cookie into his mouth. "A better choice would have been to get more of them."

"I read somewhere that you get a hundred percent satisfaction from your first bite of something, and by the third bite, you're just eating it because it's there."

Trevor slanted a glance at the cookie in her hand and calculated that, at best, she'd taken three bites. "Then you can give me yours."

"What? No!" Lucy moved away from him, melodramatically shielding the cookie in her hand. "This is mine, and you can't have it."

"Simply trying to be helpful." Trevor offered a bland smile. "Wouldn't want you eating something just for the sake of eating it."

"You worry about your own—" Lucy stopped. "Is yours already gone?"

His lips lifted in a satisfied smile. "Yes, and I enjoyed every single bite."

"Well…" Lucy finished off hers in several bites. "Mine is history, too."

Trevor chuckled, finding everything about her endearing, from the tiny crumbs dusting her upper lip to the good-natured sparring.

He'd dated Anna Beth for over a year and had planned to marry her. In this moment, he realized that he'd never felt fully at ease around her.

Not her fault, but his. It struck him that throughout their courtship he'd pretended to be someone else, someone like her and her family. He'd glossed over his family history, including the fact that his mother had preferred partying and men to spending time with him and that he'd had to fend for himself since he'd been twelve.

Keeping those feelings hidden had put a wedge between them.

She'd felt the distance and made the assumption he didn't love her. He *had* loved her but, he realized now, not the way she deserved to be loved.

He hadn't been the man for her any more than she'd been the woman for him. Now, Lucy…

Slanting a glance in her direction, he saw that she was drinking her mocha and happily gazing at the elaborate lights on the homes in this area.

She'd taken off her hat, and that glorious blonde hair was like a golden cloud around her shoulders.

Trevor turned onto another street, and the yards on this block were filled with inflatables. Santa took top honors, followed by Frosty and, Trevor's personal favorite, an inflatable red and green dragon.

"I must be too much of a traditionalist," Lucy commented. "The dragon might be more cute than creepy, but he doesn't say Christmas to me."

"I bet the kids love him."

"You're probably right." Lucy cast one more glance at the dragon before they turned the corner, and then she refocused on Trevor.

The block he'd turned down was dark. No trees blasting light through front windows, no homes with yard decorations. "It's like no one on this block cares enough to decorate."

"Those who live here might not have gotten around to it yet." Lucy's tone remained offhand. "It's still early in the season."

Trevor slowed to almost a stop on the deserted street, then turned to face her. "Do you have your lights and tree up?"

"I have lights around my front window." Her lips twitched as if she tried not to smile. "You thought I was going to say I have nothing up, and then you were going to call me a Grinch."

Trevor laughed. "You know me so well."

"I'm starting to." She smiled. "No matter how busy I am, I

always have lights around the window. I put them up last week when it was nice out."

"Any inflatables in the yard?"

Lucy shook her head. "I'm saving that kind of stuff for when I have kids."

"You want children?"

"I do." She didn't even need time to think about that answer. "Does that surprise you?"

"A little," he admitted. "I mean, I want kids someday, but I guess I never thought you did."

Puzzlement blanketed her pretty face. "I don't understand why."

"You work hard and are dedicated to making the Barns a success."

"True, but lots of people work hard and still find time for a home and family." Lucy's expression turned thoughtful. "I've not had much work-home balance the past few years, but that's on me. And that's going to change. I'm going to make time for what's important."

"Like driving around looking at Christmas lights?" He'd said it as a joke, but she didn't laugh or even smile.

"Like spending time with those who matter to me."

Trevor swallowed hard against the lump rising in his throat. He slanted a glance in her direction before starting down the road. Snow had begun to fall, and he could tell by the size of the flakes that it was going to accumulate.

"Like you, I've spent most of the past few years working on building my career, sometimes to the detriment of my personal life." He shook his head. "So far, the time I've spent here is the longest I've gone without working."

"You haven't worked on anything at all?"

His lips lifted in a slow smile. "I may have done some carving on Christmas gifts."

"I went to your website. The pieces I looked at are…amazing."

"Thank you." It touched him that she'd taken the time to do that and that she liked what she'd seen. He was tempted to tell her that one of the pieces he was working on was for her, but he stopped himself, wanting it to be a surprise. "Where to now?"

"Well, I suppose I should get home." Lucy covered a yawn with two fingers. "The morning is going to come all too soon."

"I've enjoyed our time together." Trevor tossed the words out there in as casual a voice as he could manage. "We'll have to do it again sometime."

"Yes." Lucy smiled at him. "Yes, we definitely will."

As Trevor turned in the direction of downtown, where Lucy's car was parked, he wondered if she considered this a date.

He didn't ask, because he'd meant what he'd told her. Whatever this was between them could be whatever she wanted it to be.

CHAPTER THIRTEEN

With each passing day, the sizzle between Lucy and Trevor threatened to explode into a full-blown fire.

Darrelle Peters, the woman coordinating the Burton Coffee Roasters party details, had been in daily contact. Not only was Lucy arranging the catering and all the decorations, she'd been tasked with booking rooms for those who wanted to stay overnight in Holly Pointe after the big two-day event ended on the eighteenth.

The parties scheduled in the Baby Barn for Friday and Saturday through the rest of the year had Lucy doing a happy dance. Right now, the only dates open were for Christmas Eve and Christmas Day, and those were dates she refused to fill. Her employees needed that time to be with their family and friends.

Lucy spent the next hour going through all the figures and making certain that there would be no surprises when she applied for her business loan in January.

She knew exactly the minimum amount of money she would need to put down to qualify for a loan that would pay her mother what she wanted for the Barns at Grace Hollow.

Lucy did a couple of stretches to relax the tense muscles in her neck and upper back. She'd been sitting for too long, hunched over her laptop, studying figures until her eyes bled.

Well, enough was enough. With efficient movements, she cleared her desk and stowed her laptop. She decided to head up the stairs to the studio apartment her mother had added to the initial plans when the Big Barn had been built.

After Kevin's death, Lucy had seriously considered moving from the house she'd shared with him into the six-hundred-square foot space. In the end, she'd scrapped the idea. Remaining in the home they'd shared brought her comfort. The only time she used the apartment was if the weather was bad, or if she worked late and didn't feel like driving home.

For now, the weather, always an unknown, had cooperated. A few storms had swept through, dropping several inches of snow. Child's play for the snow-removal equipment in this part of the country.

Even if the winter months ended up being snowier than usual, Lucy was glad she didn't live in the apartment. She had the feeling the proximity to work would make it difficult for her to separate herself from the job. Like she'd told Trevor, her goal was a healthy work-home balance.

If she lived this close, it would be too easy to simply just slip down the stairs and check on how events were going or how her employees were handling things.

Today, she'd been working since six a.m. She needed—no, deserved—a break. She'd just bent over to stretch her back muscles when a knock sounded at the door.

Lucy slowly straightened. "Come in."

"You don't care who it is?" Trevor smiled that slow smile and her heart did a flip. "It's just, 'Come in, one and all'?"

"It's a business office in the heart of a huge event venue." Lucy's own smile came easy. "I'm perfectly safe."

His gaze scanned her clean desk and the laptop in a bag propped up against the desk. "Ready to call it a day?"

"Thinking about it." Lucy ran a hand through her hair and expelled a heavy breath.

"Any plans for the evening?"

"Depends." She shot him an impish smile. "Who wants to know?"

Trevor studied her face for a long moment. "I have a proposition for you."

"Ohhh, a proposition. I like the sound of that."

For a second, their eyes met, and a slow burn started in the pit of Lucy's stomach and traveled outward. There were many different types of propositions, but only one came to mind when she looked at Trevor.

He took a step closer to her.

She took a step closer to him.

Barely a foot separated them when the door was flung open.

"Lucy, I'm glad I caught you."

Trevor didn't jump back, and Lucy was grateful for that fact. Nothing said *guilty* like a quick movement. She turned toward the young woman.

"What can I help you with, Kins?"

Kinsley slanted a glance at Trevor.

She'd come to Holly Pointe after Trevor had left, so Lucy quickly performed the introductions, adding, "Trevor and I go way back. You can say whatever you need to say in front of him."

The look of startled surprise on Kinsley's face likely alerted Trevor that Lucy giving permission for Kinsley to speak freely in the presence of a nonemployee wasn't common.

"Francis Dobbs, the emu guy…" Kinsley's lips pressed together for a couple of seconds. "Mr. Dobbs feels strongly that since we allowed him to exhibit, and he paid his exhibit fee plus extra to allow Pretty in his booth, we should view Pretty's destruction as a cost of doing business. Which means, in his opinion, he doesn't owe us a dime."

"Pretty?" Trevor asked.

"The emu," Lucy said at the same time as Kinsley.

"I'm sorry you had to deal with him, Kins." Sympathy filled Lucy's voice. "It sounds like he was a jerk."

"Not a full-on jerk, but definitely condescending." Kinsley's red lips tipped upward. "I think he called me 'little girl' three or four times. I was tempted to call him 'old man,' but I refrained."

"I'll call him back."

"What are you going to tell him?"

Lucy admired this quality in the woman she was considering for Hedy's old job. Though Kinsley was fresh out of college, she was eager to learn, not to mention dependable. "I plan to point to the specific section of the contract he signed that clearly states that this type of damage is the exhibitor's responsibility. If he doesn't agree, I'll refer him to our lawyer."

"I can call him back if you'd like."

Lucy started to say she could handle it, until she realized that this was something Kinsley could manage. After pulling a pencil and notepad from her desk, Lucy wrote down the section in the agreement as well as their lawyer's name.

Though she didn't glance at Trevor, and he hadn't spoken since his question about Pretty, she felt him watching the interaction between her and Kinsley.

"Either tell him we've spoken and discussed the matter, or simply say you researched his concern, and this is what you discovered." Lucy handed the sheet of paper to Kinsley. "If he still balks at paying, give him our attorney's name and tell him we'll be in touch."

"Got it." Kinsley turned to smile at Trevor. "Nice to meet you."

Then she was gone, leaving Lucy and Trevor once again alone. "Where were we?" Lucy asked.

"She's lucky to have you."

"What do you mean? Who?"

"Kinsley. You used this as a teachable moment for your employee and trusted her to handle the situation. Lots of employers would have taken it on themselves and made her feel incompetent."

"I worked for my mother for several years before she decided running the Barns was too much work and turned over the operations management to me." Lucy's tips quirked up in a wry smile. "I believe she taught me how not to do things as much as she did how to do them."

Trevor laughed. "If Paula is anything like my mother, I'd say that's likely an accurate statement."

"Now, back to where we were."

It was perhaps an unfortunate—or maybe a fortunate—choice of words, as they both knew they'd been about to kiss. There wasn't a single doubt in Lucy's mind that's what would have happened if Kinsley hadn't arrived.

Trevor's lips lifted in a slow smile.

Though she was seriously tempted to take a step forward, she was conscious of Kinsley being in the outer office only several feet away, which kept Lucy's feet firmly planted where she was. She arched an eyebrow. "You said you have a proposition?"

"Oh yeah. I know you haven't had a chance to get your tree up yet. I thought maybe tonight, after we're done here, we could grab a pizza, get a tree, and I'll help you decorate it."

For a second, Lucy didn't know what to say. This wasn't at all what she'd expected. Then again, had she really thought he'd press her to sleep with him when she'd made it clear that wasn't what she wanted?

The trouble was, she had started to want him, but wasn't sure how to tell him she'd changed her mind.

"If you don't want to, I understand." He spoke quickly into the silence that she'd allowed to stretch far too long.

"I think it sounds like fun."

The grin he shot her arrowed straight to her heart. "Yeah?"

"Yeah." She thought quickly of the logistics. "Why don't you pick me up at my house at seven? It'll be dark by then, but the tree lot is well lit."

"That works."

Lucy's phone buzzed. She pulled it out and glanced down. "It looks like Austin needs some help in the Marketplace. Are you—?"

"I'm on it." Before he turned to go, he stepped to her. Placing his hands on her shoulders, Trevor kissed her softly on the lips, then headed out the door, whistling.

～

As Lucy had contemplated the evening ahead, she'd realized that while decorating the tree and sharing a pizza with Trevor sounded like a whole lot of fun, there was something she wanted more.

She wanted him. If the heat in his eyes when he looked at her was any indication, he wanted her just as badly.

While waiting for him, Lucy picked up the house, refreshed her makeup, then spritzed on some perfume.

She put candles on the table for their dinner of pizza and wine, then promptly put the candles away, feeling foolish.

At the tree lot, there were lots of trees to choose from, but the fir they ended up choosing was the perfect size and shape for her small living room.

Trevor placed it in the tree stand while she put the pizza in the oven and poured them each a glass of wine.

She'd just turned on the oven light to monitor the pizza's progress when Trevor strode into the room.

"It smells good already." The words had barely left his lips when he wrapped his arms around her from behind, his breath a soft caress on her neck. He sniffed. "Now, you... You smell amazing."

Her heart suddenly squeezed tight in her chest. Lucy leaned back against his hard, firm body and sighed. "This is nice."

When Trevor turned her in his arms, Lucy placed her hands on his shoulders. "This is nice, too." With the tips of her fingers, she touched the scruff on his angular jaw. "Sexy."

His gaze traveled slowly over her face, then as if finding the answer to the question he hadn't voiced, he closed his mouth over hers. He tasted as good as he smelled.

Her control nearly shattered as his hand flattened against her lower back, drawing her up against the length of his body. She felt the evidence of his desire for her, and a smoldering heat flared through her, a sensation she didn't want to fight.

Why should she fight? She wanted this man. Wanted to run her hands over his body, to feel the coiled strength of muscle sliding under her fingers.

His kiss might have started out as sweet as the ones they'd shared before, but she felt his need and knew it matched her own.

"I want you, Lucy." He might have voiced the comment as a statement, but she heard the question.

She smiled and trailed a finger down his cheek, her eyes never leaving his. "I want you, too."

The timer on the oven dinged.

Without stepping from his arms, Lucy reached over and shut off the oven.

"Do you need to take care of that?" he asked in a husky voice that made her blood feel like warm honey sliding through her veins.

"Nope." Smiling, and feeling a little shy, she took his hand and led him to her bedroom.

When they stood next to the bed, he pulled her to him and caught her mouth in a hard, deep kiss.

Her eyes fluttered shut as she gave in to the sensations, but when she opened them, she saw the Christmas pillowcases. The ones Kevin had given her.

Trevor's hand was under her shirt, the tips of his fingers nearly to her aching breast, when she grabbed his wrist. "Stop."

He froze and dropped his hand to his side as Lucy took a step back. She raked her hands through her hair, an ache of longing still racking her body. "I'm sorry."

Those warm brown eyes settled on hers. "What's wrong?"

"The pillowcases." She pushed out the words between trembling lips. "They were a gift from—"

She didn't finish, didn't want to bring Kevin into this room, though he was already here.

"I get it," he said, smoothing the moisture from her cheeks with the tips of his fingers.

Only then did Lucy realize tears were slipping down her cheeks.

"You do?"

"I can understand feeling awkward in the house you shared with Kevin, because I'd feel the same way if we were at Gran's house." Trevor's lips quirked upward. "That wouldn't be particularly conducive to a romantic evening."

"But I want you." She glanced again at the bed. "Maybe if I put the pillows in another room…"

"Luce, listen. As much as I want you, I don't think this is the place." His gaze searched hers. "Not tonight, anyway. And if it's just that you're not ready, I'm totally okay with that, too."

"I am ready. Just not—"

"Here. Got it." He wrapped his arms around her and kissed her forehead. "What say we grab some pizza and decorate the tree?"

"But what about—?"

"The other? Well, I've got an idea." He smiled. "Leave that to me."

CHAPTER FOURTEEN

Trevor's idea, it turned out, was a romantic dinner in Burlington. When he'd asked her this morning if it would work for her to leave work at six and not return until around noon on Wednesday, Lucy had spoken with Kins and Austin and made it happen.

Her overnight bag was in the back seat of Trevor's truck. On the drive, he'd told her he'd made reservations at the hotel next to where they would have dinner. If she decided she wanted to go straight home after they ate, no worries.

Lucy glanced around the interior of the Hen of the Wood. The farm-to-table restaurant, known for amazing culinary creations, reminded her a lot of the Barns at Grace Hollow with its geometric wood-beam ceilings and barn aesthetic.

The shiny top of the hickory table where they sat might not be covered in a linen cloth, but that didn't make the restaurant seem any less elegant.

"This place is gorgeous." She took a sip of the wine she'd ordered, glad she'd chosen to dress up for an evening out.

"You're the one who is gorgeous." Trevor reached across the table and took her hand, his fingers playing with hers. "I'm so happy this worked out."

"I'm so happy you made reservations." Lucy chuckled. "If you hadn't, I think we'd still be waiting."

They'd arrived a few minutes early for their reservation at six and found the place nearly full.

"I'm glad, too, but waiting wouldn't have been a problem. Just being with you is enough." Trevor gave her hand a squeeze and took another roll. "These Parker House rolls taste pretty good."

"I think it's the cultured butter that makes the difference."

"Whatever it is, it's good."

She wondered if all the small talk they'd been doing since they'd been seated was his way of helping her to relax and not think about what would happen after they finished with their meal.

"What's that look about?" he asked.

"What look?"

"You're frowning."

She chuckled. "I don't mean to frown. I was just thinking about later…"

"Hey…" His hand was back on hers, and she curved her fingers around it. "I meant what I told you before we left Holly Pointe. No pressure. We can enjoy our meal, then head home. All up to you."

Lucy opened her mouth to speak, but shut it when the server returned with their heirloom salads. Once the young man stepped away, Lucy lowered her voice. "I don't want to go back after the meal."

Even in the dim light, she saw the flash of desire in his dark eyes. Her heart gave a solid thump against her ribs.

"The thing is, it's, well, it's been a long time for me." She gave an embarrassed chuckle. "You're going to need to keep your expectations low."

When he opened his mouth, she held up a hand and continued. "Please don't say it's like riding a bike, because the two aren't anything alike."

Trevor laughed aloud, causing the couple at a nearby table to turn and stare.

"It's not funny," she hissed.

"I know." His fingers tightened on hers when she tried to jerk back. "I'm sorry."

She gave up trying when his thumb began to caress her palm. A languid warmth filled her body, and her worry began to fade.

"There will be no disappointment, and if you feel at all uneasy or unsure, that will be all on me." The look in his eyes was one of promise. "I want to show you how much you mean to me. I have no expectations or goals beyond that. Trust me, Luce, trust me to make it good for you."

Lucy took him at his word. She relaxed and enjoyed the rest of the scrumptious meal. The rib eye for two with preserved peach jus was melt-in-your-mouth amazing, while the mushroom toast surprised them both. By the time they finished the main course, Lucy didn't think she could eat another bite.

The rhubarb sorbet with crumbled oats caught her eye. Trevor went with the truffle.

"Did you know I have several rhubarb plants in my backyard?" Lucy asked Trevor, then immediately realized the ridiculousness of the question.

"I didn't know that." Trevor smiled.

The softness in his eyes told her that he recognized her worry-meter was on the rise now that the dinner portion of the evening was nearing an end.

"I'm sorry," she said.

"No." He shook his head, his gaze never leaving her face. "I can't recall the last time I enjoyed a dinner so much."

"The food was fabulous," she admitted.

"It wasn't the food, though you're right that it's very good. I simply enjoyed being with you, talking with you, laughing with you. I just, well, it's been fun."

"Is there anything else I can get either of you?" The waiter appeared tableside with the check.

"I think we're good," Trevor told him.

"You've been wonderful." Lucy smiled at the young man. "Thank you for taking such good care of us."

Us.

The word came so easily to her lips now. Somehow, over the past month, Trevor had found a way into her heart. From the way he looked at her, from what he said, she'd found her way into his.

At that moment, Lucy realized she really was no longer content with a few stolen kisses whenever they could manage to be alone. She wanted Trevor, and she wanted him tonight.

"I'm glad we came here." Lucy took Trevor's arm when they left the restaurant. She glanced back at the rustic stone façade frontage. "We'll have to come back."

"Definitely."

The brilliant smile Trevor flashed had heat coursing through her veins. She pointed to the Hotel Vermont, conveniently located right next to Hen of the Wood. "Is that where we have reservations?"

"It is." His gaze never left her face.

"Well, then, I think it's time we checked in."

While Trevor turned on the gas fireplace in the room, Lucy explored the room in the ultramodern hotel that still managed to have a woodsy vibe.

The so-called Whirlpool King Bedroom on the top floor boasted not only a gas fireplace, but a jetted whirlpool tub. Candles were on the edge of the tub, along with an ice bucket that held an unopened bottle of champagne.

Trevor turned to her, and a tentative smile lifted his lips when he caught her staring. He spoke cautiously. "Is everything okay?"

She offered an unsteady smile as she gestured with one hand around the room. "Did you do all this?"

"Do all what?" he asked in a halting voice, his gaze watchful.

"Make this so perfect." Lucy stepped to him then, wrapping her arms around him and breathing in the clean, fresh scent that she'd come to associate with him.

"I want tonight to be perfect for you, Luce." He gave a stran-gled-sounding chuckle. "I want every time you're with me to be perfect."

Her heart swelled to bursting as she cupped his face in her hands. "That's how it is for me when I'm with you—perfect."

Then she pressed her lips to his, and everything around them faded until all she knew was that being with him, right here, right now, was exactly where she was meant to be.

Trevor hadn't expected his grandmother to be sitting in the living room when he strolled through the door the next morning.

"How was the slumber party at Mary's?" He dropped into the chair nearest hers.

"It was wonderful." Hedy's lips curved. "We played cards, ate, talked, ate some more. I can't recall having a better time."

He cocked his head. "But you're already home."

"The one thing we didn't do was get much sleep." Hedy covered a yawn with her fingers. "I told Mary this morning that I had to go home and get some rest. By the time I left, the house was already filled with people."

"Who brought you home?" Trevor pulled out his phone. No missed calls.

"Ginny Blain. She was going right by here."

Trevor knew Ginny, Holly Pointe's expert on building gingerbread houses. She was also one of Mary's best friends.

"That was nice of her." Trevor nearly said he'd have gotten home earlier if he'd known Hedy would be there. But the truth was, he'd enjoyed being with Lucy too much to cut short any of the time he'd spent with her.

Just remembering the night they'd shared had a smile lifting his lips.

"I manage quite well on my own." Hedy's gaze turned thoughtful. "That doesn't mean I don't enjoy having you around. I did find myself wondering where you were."

Trevor cast aside thoughts of Lucy to focus on his grandmother. "Lucy and I had dinner at Hen of the Wood in Burlington and spent the evening together."

By the assessing look in her eyes, he saw instantly that he'd come up short.

Hedy gestured toward the hall where the bedrooms were in the home. "When I went by your bedroom on my way to the bathroom this morning, I noticed your bed hadn't been slept in."

Trevor owed his grandmother honesty, but he also felt loyalty toward Lucy. If she wanted Hedy to know that they'd spent the night together, Lucy would need to be the one to tell her.

"Have you been to Hen of the Wood?" Trevor deliberately focused on the food portion of the evening.

"I have not," Hedy admitted. "I hear it's excellent."

"The food is amazing." Trevor's lips curved. "It's been a long time since I've enjoyed a meal more."

"The person you were with may have had something to do with that," Hedy said with a knowing smile.

"True." Trevor smiled. "Lucy and I… We never seem to run out of things to say."

Hedy continued to study him with her inscrutable blue eyes. "What's next?"

Trevor knew what his grandmother was asking, and he knew what he wanted. He wanted it all with Lucy. "That's up to her."

"You like her."

Trevor nodded. "What I feel for Lucy goes far beyond like. I love her, Gran."

"I'm happy for both of you." A softness filled Hedy's eyes. "Lucy has been alone for far too long, and so have you."

It would be easy, too easy, Trevor knew, to get caught up in thinking that this thing with Lucy could go the distance. Heck, even right now, he found himself considering how he could move his workshop to Holly Pointe. But there was one big obstacle that neither he nor his grandmother had brought up.

The elephant in the room. This elephant had a name—Kevin Johnson.

"Lucy loves Kevin." Trevor pushed to his feet, unable to sit any longer.

"Kevin is dead," Hedy reminded him.

"Don't you think I know that?" he snapped, then felt immediately contrite. Taking a deep breath, he brought his emotions under better control. "I'm sorry, Gran. It's just that we both know that while Kevin may be gone from this world, he's still front and center in her heart."

"A ghost, a memory, can't keep you warm on a cold winter's night."

"No," Trevor agreed. "But it can keep you from fully opening your heart and loving another man in the here and now."

Normally, with only a little over three weeks left before Christmas, Lucy would have worked through her lunch hour. But she'd begun to realize the importance of taking time for herself.

Besides, things were flowing smoothly at Grace Hollow this bright and sunny Thursday. The Marketplace bustled with buyers, and the Baby Barn was all set up for a local writers group Christmas party later in the afternoon.

Lunch at Jingle Shells with her friends had been on the calendar for several weeks. Eleven had been chosen as the time to meet so they would be assured of getting a table.

Lucy walked through the front door of the café at eleven on the nose. She saw her friends sitting at a table by the window.

Kate, dressed casually in jeans and a kelly-green sweater, made a pretty picture against the window decorated with vinyl clings of snowflakes in varying sizes and shapes along with a large upside-down Rudolph.

Mel wore what Lucy thought of as her Christmas shirt, with "Rosie's Makes Everything Merry and Bright" in glittery letters across the front.

Stella kept glancing toward the doorway, as if keeping an eye out for Lucy.

Lucy lifted her hand, and Stella smiled and returned the wave.

"Looks like I'm the last one to arrive." As there were two empty seats at the round table near the window, Lucy took the one where she could look out over the dining area. "Why the round?"

"All the four-tops were already taken." Mel, an experienced server, spoke with authority. "They didn't want to push two of the deuces together."

Kate placed her hand on the top of the chair next to her. "That may be partially true, but I like to think that even though Faith isn't here with us today, she's here in spirit."

Stella laughed. "C'mon, she's not dead. She's in New York City."

"That doesn't keep me from wishing she was here with us." Kate ruined her serious tone when she grinned.

Lucy picked up the menu and glanced around the table, remembering when Trevor had brought her lunch. "What's everyone having?"

"I can't decide." Stella heaved a breath. "Everything sounds good."

"That's what I was thinking," Kate lamented. "I almost wish they had fewer choices."

The server, dressed in a long-sleeved tee that displayed the words "Easily Distracted by Jingle Shells," along with images of the wide variety of pasta shells served in the café, stopped at the table.

Lucy gestured. "Cute shirt."

The young man's lips—he couldn't have been more than eighteen—lifted in a good-natured grin. "It's pretty chill for a work shirt."

Kate's gaze scanned the group. "Do we need more time?"

"I can come back," the young man offered.

Lucy had seen the customers streaming into the café and knew it'd take a while for him to come back. "Do you still have that sampler platter? The one that contains a little bit of each of the main menu items?"

"It's on our evening menu, but I think I can get it for you." He gestured with one hand. "My manager is right over there. Do you want me to check with him?"

"That'd be great," Lucy told him.

"Be right back." He hurried off.

"A week or so ago, Trevor brought me a sampler platter from here." Lucy counted the entrees off on her fingers. "It had Fa- La-La-Lasagna, Fettuccini Alfred-Ho-Ho-Ho, spaghetti with meatballs and Good King Wence-Sauce, Linguine with Santa Claws and Frosty the Sno-Manicotti. It was a lot of food, and it'd be more than enough for the four of us to share."

Before any of her friends could comment, the server was back. "She says we can do it."

"Just a suggestion," Lucy told her friends.

"Sounds good to me," Stella said, and Mel and Kate nodded.

It wasn't long before the food was on the table. Talk revolved initially around upcoming events, including the party Dustin and Krista were throwing at their cabin.

"Trevor asked me to go with him." Lucy didn't think it was a big pronouncement, but for a second all forks stilled.

"Are you going to do it?" Mel asked.

"Lucy's already gone out with him once," Kate reminded her. "You know she doesn't do second dates."

"I saw her with him at the tree lighting." Stella spoke casually.

"Pastor Mann told me he saw you and Trevor buying a tree at Landers on Monday," Mel said with a slight smile.

"Is it true?" Curiosity sparked in Kate's green depths.

"All true." Lucy couldn't keep from smiling. "In fact, earlier this week, we went to Burlington and had dinner at Hen of the Wood." Lucy had planned to stop there, but her mouth had other ideas. "Then we capped off the date with a night at the Hotel Vermont."

"Hallelujah! It's about time you got back out there. How was it?" Kate smiled broadly. "Does this mean he's moving back for good?"

"Do you want this to be going anywhere?" Mel's gaze met hers. "Does he?"

Stella searched her face. "Are you happy?"

"I don't really have answers. I wasn't expecting this." Lucy stirred her pasta with her fork. "I'd never felt ready to date, much less sleep with anyone, since Kevin. But Trevor just kind of happened, and yeah, I am happy. I don't know where it's going or what he wants."

Mel twirled spaghetti around her fork. "Can't you just ask?"

Kate laughed. "Right, because every guy wants to hear, 'So what's our future?' right after sex."

"She doesn't have to ask it that way," Mel protested. "It's important to make sure you're on the same page. If he wants something serious—"

"Who wouldn't want something serious with Lucy?" Kate took a sip of iced tea. "Our girl is a catch."

"She absolutely is, but does she want to be caught?" Mel slanted a questioning glance at Lucy. "All I'm saying is, it's better to know sooner rather than later if you want different things."

Stella lifted a hand. "Let's all relax and give Lucy time to take a breath. Sweetie, you don't have to ask him anything you don't want to right now. You can just be with him and enjoy yourself. All that matters is you're happy. That's what we all want for you, including Sam and the whole family."

CHAPTER FIFTEEN

Lucy shot a sideways glance at Trevor as they climbed the steps to Dustin and Krista's cabin the following Friday. This week, they'd had lunch at Rosie's, gone sledding with a group at Dobson's Hill and taken part in pond hockey on Wednesday night.

Now, here they were, attending a party together. Lucy couldn't remember having a better week.

Trevor looked positively yummy in dark pants and a sweater. Lucy, who liked to use any opportunity to wear a dress, had chosen a red sweater dress paired with tights and boots.

Channeling her inner Faith Pierson, a friend who always shone in outfits that drew the eye, Lucy had pulled her hair back on top and tied it with a wide white ribbon edged in red that had short, squatty Santas ho-ho-hoing.

When they reached the front steps, Lucy slipped her arm around Trevor's arm.

Turning to her, he smiled.

"I'm glad we came together." She brushed her lips against his cheek, then gave a breathless squeal when he pulled her to him and kissed her on the mouth.

Lucy was still slightly breathless when the door opened.

Krista and Dustin stood together, welcoming smiles on their faces.

"Lucy." Krista pulled her inside.

Dustin shook Trevor's hand. "Glad you could make it."

"Thanks for the invitation," Trevor said.

"I look forward to your parties every year." Lucy gave Krista and then Dustin a hug.

"We look forward to having you," Dustin said, then shifted his focus to Trevor. "I've been meaning to reach out. Krista and I are working on a new idea, a show that is a woodworking/design competition, and we'd like you to be involved."

Trevor cocked his head. "What would I be doing?"

"Most likely, you'd be working as a technical adviser," Dustin told him.

"We're still working out the details." Krista, dressed casually in black pants, heels and a fluffy white sweater, still managed to look elegant. She slipped her arm through her husband's and kissed his cheek. "I thought we weren't going to talk business tonight."

"What you're proposing sounds interesting." Trevor smiled. "Let me know when you've worked out the details."

"For now, you two mingle and have fun." Krista touched Lucy's arm. "You look amazing. We'll talk later, and you can tell me where you got that dress."

When another couple arrived, Lucy and Trevor stepped deeper into the cabin.

Trevor's gaze swept the large space on the main level. Along with the soaring ceilings, the entire back wall of windows added an openness to the room. The hearth of the rustic fireplace held a roaring fire, while a chandelier of antlers drew the eye overhead. "I don't think I've ever been in a cabin this nice."

"You know what I like about it?" Lucy stepped close, placing a hand on Trevor's arm, wanting to make sure he could hear her.

"What?"

The smile he bestowed on her had everything in Lucy melting. "Despite its size and grandeur, it still has a homey feel."

Trevor thought for a moment, then nodded. "Like Hedy's house."

"Right." She smiled, pleased he'd understood.

"I believe that feeling has a lot to do with the people who live here." His gaze met hers. "The love that exists inside these four walls."

"That's probably a big part of it." As they made their way to the bar, Lucy found herself wondering what it would be like to share a house with Trevor, to share a life with Trevor.

The thought had excitement coursing through her and brought back that breathless feeling.

While they waited for the bartender to pour their drinks, Trevor's hand slipped around her waist in a gesture that seemed familiar, as if he'd been doing it for years.

Since making love, they had developed an ease with each other that hadn't been there before—like the kiss they'd shared before Krista and Dustin opened the door.

Sometimes, Lucy thought, she felt like a hormone-riddled teenager. Or, probably more accurately, like a woman falling in love.

"Lucy."

A smile was on her lips, her wineglass in hand, when she turned toward Stella's voice. Sam was with her, of course. It seemed the two were always together.

"Stella. Sam." Instead of hugs, Lucy settled for a bright smile. "It's so good to see you."

"I'm not sure I should speak to you." Sam shook his head. "Not after Wednesday."

"What happened Wednesday?" Despite her best efforts, Lucy's voice rose.

"You picked this guy," Sam gestured at Trevor with his head, "to be on your team instead of me. And then, when Dustin, Mr. NHL MVP, showed up late, you got him on your team—"

"Because we were playing one short," Lucy reminded him, seeing the tiny smile hovering at the corners of Sam's lips. "Not my fault you couldn't get the biscuit into the net."

A startled look crossed Stella's face. "Biscuit?"

"Puck," Sam, Lucy and Trevor answered at the same time.

"Phew." Stella pretended to wipe sweat from her brow. "For a moment, I envisioned a buttermilk biscuit flying into the net, spewing crumbs everywhere."

Sam laughed and kissed her. "There's that Florida girl in you coming out."

Stella smiled up at her husband. "Well, this Florida girl would like a ginger ale."

"The wine selection is excellent," Lucy told her, knowing she and Stella both loved dry red wines. She held out her glass. "The Pinot Noir is amazing."

"I'm off wine—actually, alcohol—for the duration." Stella looked up at her husband. "Sam offered to do the same, but I told him, 'Not necessary.'"

"You're not drinking—" It suddenly hit Lucy. "Omigod, Stella, are you and Sam pregnant?"

Stella smiled. "We are. Just got the confirmation this morning."

"Congratulations." Trevor's gaze shifted from Sam to Stella. "You'll be great parents."

"We talked about," for a second, Stella's confident tone faltered, "naming him Kevin if it's a boy. I didn't know Kevin, but he sounds like a wonderful man, and Sam thought—"

"I thought this would be a way to honor him." Sam's gaze met Lucy's. "I don't want it to be awkward, so if you'd prefer we didn't—"

"It's a wonderful tribute." Lucy placed a hand on Sam's arm. "I believe Kevin would be honored."

"We haven't told my family yet that we're pregnant." Sam lowered his tone. "We're planning to tell them Sunday, so if you can keep this just between us?"

"Of course." Lucy could only imagine Geoff and Emily's reaction to the news. "They're going to be thrilled."

As they spent several minutes chatting about babies, something Lucy knew little to nothing about, she could feel Trevor's eyes on her.

Once Sam and Stella stepped away, he turned to her.

"Seriously, would it bother you?"

"Seriously, no." Lucy took Trevor's hand, loving the warmth in the large fingers that wrapped around hers. "I'd have said if it would. I think it'd be nice."

He only nodded.

"I noticed you didn't have much to say," she commented.

"It was over my head." Trevor shook his head. "When the baby talk started, I didn't have a clue about any of it."

"When it's our turn, we'll have to hit the online research." The second the words left her lips, Lucy realized by the way she'd phrased the comment, she might have given him the wrong impression.

"We will." Trevor agreed. "And we'll have Hedy."

Lucy didn't know what to say to that. Was he assuming that they'd have kids together? Or merely commenting that Hedy would be a good resource if either of them had children in another relationship?

Not wanting to dig herself into a hole she couldn't get out of, Lucy only nodded her agreement and changed the subject.

"Sam and Stella spend a lot of time together."

Trevor took a sip of beer. "They enjoy each other's company."

Simple as that. Not complicated at all.

You enjoy someone's company, you spend time with them.

That's how it had been for her and Trevor this week. She'd

seen him every day. Looking back, it felt as if they'd crammed a month's worth of activities into each week he'd been back.

Lucy had wondered if they'd get sick of each other. Instead, it had been quite the opposite for her. The more she was with Trevor, the more she wanted to be with him.

That's how it was when you were in love. It was how it had been with Kevin, she remembered.

"I enjoy your company," she told him.

"Same goes." His gaze searched hers. "Is it just me, or has it been forever since we've been alone?"

She leaned over and lightly brushed his lips with hers. "It's been forever. I'd suggest we leave, but the thing is, I haven't been to many parties. I'm good at organizing events, but not as good— or maybe I should say comfortable—at simply being a guest. Tonight is a kind of new beginning for me. I'd like to mingle for a while longer, then we can go somewhere more…private."

"Sure. But when we are ready to leave, where will we go?"

He might have asked the question, but Lucy could almost see the wheels turning in his head as he considered and rejected options.

"We'll figure out something."

"How long—?" he began, but stopped when a gentleman Lucy recognized as Dustin's father stopped to say hello.

"Mr. Bellamy." Lucy's smile came easily. She'd always liked Terry Bellamy. And Krista's parents, too, for that matter. Both couples were frequent visitors to Holly Pointe, especially since their children spent most Christmas holidays here. "It's so good to see you."

"Dianna and I drove to the Barns today and strolled around the Marketplace." Terry cast a curious look in Trevor's direction before returning his attention to Lucy. "The place was busy. I hear you're in the process of buying the business. When will that transfer take place?"

Lucy wondered where Terry had heard about the pending sale, then decided it didn't matter. It was hardly a secret.

"Pending loan approval, the plan is to close on the deal at the end of January." Before Terry could ask any more questions, Lucy put a hand on Trevor's arm and performed the introductions.

"I know it was a long time ago," Terry said, "but I remember you being at some pond hockey games when we used to come here for the holidays."

"I remember Dustin being the one we absolutely had to have on our team if we hoped to have any chance of winning." Trevor shook his head, a tiny smile playing at the corners of his lips. "Your son was a force to be reckoned with, even in grade school."

"That he was." Terry turned to Lucy. "Dustin said something about Geoff and Emily being in town. I thought they might be here tonight. Dianna and I always enjoy visiting with them."

From where she stood, Lucy had a view of the front door, and when the bells chimed, she saw Krista hurry across the floor to greet their late-arriving guests.

Geoff Johnson, tall with dark hair and a lean athletic build, stepped through the door. The Tony-winning playwright of too many successful Broadway productions to count was what Sam would look like in another twenty-five years. Dressed in dark pants and a gray sweater, Geoff looked even more distinguished with the few strands of gray in his dark hair.

He'd grown up in Holly Pointe, but for most of his life, he'd called NYC home.

Beside him, his wife, Emily Danforth, looked gorgeous in her winter-white dress and sweater. Like Kevin had been, she was blonde. Her teal-colored scarf added a nice pop of color to all the white. A Broadway producer, she was one of those women who was at ease in any crowd.

After speaking with their host and hostess, Geoff and Emily glanced around the room. When they spotted Lucy, they crossed to her.

For many years, Lucy had thought this wonderful couple, who'd stepped into parental roles for her from the time she'd been fifteen, would be her in-laws. Every year since Kevin's death, they'd generously continued to include her in family gatherings.

"Lucy." Emily enfolded her in a hug, and the creamy vanilla scent of Dior Joy and the feel of the woman's arms were so familiar that Lucy let herself linger. "You look wonderful."

Geoff's hug came next. "It's good to see you, sweet girl."

He was the closest thing to a father she'd ever had, and Emily had taught her how loving a mother could be.

"You remember Dustin's father, Terry," Lucy began once she'd stepped back.

"Of course. It's good to see you." Geoff shifted his attention to Trevor, who stood beside Lucy. "I don't believe we've met."

"We haven't." Trevor offered Geoff a warm smile and shook his hand. "Trevor Sherwood."

"Trevor is originally from Holly Pointe." Lucy smiled at Trevor. "He's in town visiting his grandmother."

"It's good to meet you, Trevor." Geoff gave him an assessing look.

"A pleasure to meet you both." Trevor widened his smile to include Emily.

"It's so nice to see you here with someone, Lucy. We hope you two have a lovely evening together." Emily inclined her head. "Will the two of you be at Sam and Stella's on Sunday?"

It was the first Lucy had heard about the dinner, so she figured this must be when Sam and Stella planned on telling his parents the happy news. "I won't be, but I'm sure whatever they serve will be delicious. Both Sam and Stella are excellent cooks."

"Well, we should mingle." Emily wrapped her arms around Lucy for another hug and whispered in her ear, "I'm happy for you. You're so young. You deserve love."

"I love you, Em," Lucy whispered back.

"They worry about you." Trevor spoke in a low tone once they were out of earshot.

"They do," she admitted. "A little. A lot at first. Not so much now."

"Seeing you happy eases their minds."

"It does." Lucy thought of all the years they'd been such an important part of her life. "Emily was more of a mother to me than my own, and Geoff, well, he was the dad I never knew."

"They'll always be a part of your life."

Lucy had to blink back unexpected tears. He knew her so well. "Enough talk of the past. You're driving, which means I'm able to have a second glass of this amazing Pinot."

They turned in the direction of the bar, but Lucy found herself waylaid by Norma and Kenny.

"You guys catch up." Trevor squeezed her arm. "I'll be right back with your glass of Pinot."

"We'll keep her company until you return." Norma smiled warmly at Lucy. "No need to hurry."

Trevor didn't hurry. The last thing he wanted Lucy to think was that he couldn't mingle without her by his side.

Though, he had to admit, he really liked being with her.

"Hey, Trevor." Mel smiled. "If you're getting something for Lucy, the Pinot Noir is her favorite."

"That's exactly what she told me to get her." Trevor offered Mel a warm smile. "How's it going?"

"It's going good." Mel ordered a glass of wine, then turned back to Trevor. "I've been watching you and Lucy."

"What have you discovered?" Trevor kept his tone casual and offhand, not sure where Lucy's friend was headed with this.

"You like her."

Trevor grinned. "You are observant."

"I don't know if you realize it, but Lucy hasn't dated much, not since Kevin."

"She told me."

Mel gave a little laugh, but concern filled her hazel eyes. "Of course she did. I haven't seen her this happy in a long time."

Now Trevor understood. "You're worried I'll hurt her."

"Maybe even break her heart."

Irritation surged, but only for a second. Mel didn't mean to meddle—he'd put money on it. Lucy was one of her closest friends, and Mel was concerned.

About him. About his intentions.

Lucy might not have parents looking out for her, but she had friends who cared.

"I care deeply for Lucy." Though Trevor knew he loved Lucy, she needed to hear the words from him first. "I will do everything in my power to make her happy."

"You love her."

Trevor let the words hang in the air.

Mel brushed them aside with a wave of her hand. "You don't have to tell me. It's written all over your face when you talk about her. Just do me a favor?"

"If I can."

"Tell her how you feel. Otherwise, she's going to be the last to know."

CHAPTER SIXTEEN

With only three weeks left for Christmas shopping, the Marketplace was hopping. Lucy had two smaller holiday events scheduled back-to-back today in the Baby Barn.

The first was a book club luncheon and the other a dinner for a teacher who was retiring early. Once one group left, everything would need to be cleared out and readied for the evening group. Right now was the lull before the storm.

"If you don't need me anymore," Trevor said from her office doorway, "I'm going to head over to the Big Barn and see if Austin needs anything."

Lucy pushed to her feet. "I'll go with you."

"I'd love that, but who is going to watch the Baby?"

It took Lucy only a second to get the wordplay. She laughed and crossed the room to him. "You're a real comedian. You know that?"

Without giving him an opportunity to respond, she wound her arms around his neck and pressed her mouth to his for a long, sweet kiss. She dropped her head against his chest and expelled a sigh. "I thought we'd have more time for us today."

"With the Marketplace in full swing and back-to-backs in the Baby Barn, I didn't hold out much hope."

"If you're still around later…" She hesitated, then said what was on her mind. "I wish we could be together again. You know, like the night at the hotel."

"I'd like that." His arms tightened around her. "I'd like it very much, in fact."

Lifting her head, she gazed into his warm brown eyes. "You look so sexy tonight, and you smell terrific."

He glanced down at his flannel shirt and work boots, then back at her. His lips quirked upward.

"I'm glad you think so." He chuckled. "I was thinking the same about you."

The air outside might be rattling the windows, but inside her office, with his strong arms around her, Lucy felt warm and content. "I wish…"

"I know." He kissed the top of her head, then set her at arm's length. "I'll stop over after I finish at the Marketplace. Or text me when you're ready to head home."

"I'm not sure how long it will be—"

"No worries. I'll be around." He strolled with her to the office door, then leaned over and kissed her again, this time on the mouth. "You taste really good."

Lucy chuckled. "I'm not the only one."

With Trevor gone, Lucy roamed her office, feeling restless. There was so much she could be doing, but she found it difficult to concentrate.

She moved to the window and stared out into the winter wonderland of white. When she heard the office door open, she turned, a smile already on her lips.

But Trevor wasn't standing in the doorway. It was Melinda.

"I knocked, but I don't think you heard me."

Lucy was sure she'd have a heard a knock, but gave a good-natured shrug. "I guess my mind was on something else."

"Or maybe…" Mel stepped into the office and plopped down into one of the visitor chairs. "On some*one* else?"

Taking a seat in the chair next to Mel, Lucy cocked her head.

"I saw Trevor heading toward the Big Barn. He was coming from this direction."

Lucy finally understood. "He helped me get ready for the Lit 'N' Latte Book Club Christmas luncheon. Now, he's going to help Austin."

"He's been a big help to you."

"He has," Lucy agreed. "It's nice having him around."

"Have you ever asked Trevor what he is looking for?"

"Noooo." Lucy dragged out the word, everything in her going on high alert. "Why should I?"

"You two have been spending a lot of time together."

"He's helping me out around—"

"Yes, yes. He's helping you at the Barns. But you and I both know there's more going on between the two of you than work."

"Is that why you're here?" Lucy fought to keep her voice even. "To discuss Trevor?"

"Partially," Mel admitted, then flashed a smile. "I also didn't have much of a chance to speak with you last night, and since I'm not working, I thought it'd be good to catch up."

Lucy expelled the breath she hadn't realized she'd been holding. But the relief was short-lived.

"I really think you should ask Trevor what his intentions are."

"Are we back to that again already?"

Mel's eyes took on an impish gleam. "I wasn't aware we ever left."

"I haven't asked about his intentions, Mel, and I don't intend to, not right now, anyway. Why can't what Stella said be true? Why can't I just be with him without looking ahead?"

The smile that had been on Melinda's lips vanished. "Because someone will get hurt."

Lucy laughed. "I think I know a thing or two about being hurt in a relationship."

"Maybe this time it won't be you who gets hurt." Mel's expression turned solemn. "Holding tight to what used to be isn't fair to anyone."

Lucy clenched her hands in her lap and forced an even tone. "What do you mean?"

Blowing out a breath, Mel sat back, her eyes taking on a distant gleam. "You and Trevor have this connection. I feel it when you're together. Heck, I can practically see it."

Lucy offered a cautious nod. "We've become pretty good friends."

"I don't think Alex and I were ever friends—not good ones, anyway."

Alex was the man Mel had worked with and dated when she'd lived in Burlington. That had been several years ago, and Lucy hadn't gotten the whole story on what had happened.

She hadn't pressed, sensing that Mel wasn't ready to share. The subject of Alex had never been brought up. Until now.

"That surprises me." Lucy kept her tone casual. "From the little you've said, it sounded as if you and Alex were always doing stuff together."

"Do you know he contacted me?"

"He contacted you? Like, called out of the blue?"

Mel's gaze turned distant with memories. "I got a text. He said he'd been thinking about me a lot and wondered how I was doing."

Several long seconds passed while Lucy waited for Mel to elaborate. It appeared, Lucy thought, that the ball was in her court. "That was nice of him. Holiday cheer and all that."

"I wish he hadn't done that." Mel shifted in her seat toward Lucy. "It's hard."

"Because you loved him?" Lucy ventured.

"I never loved him." Mel gave a humorless laugh. "That was

the problem. After over a year of dating exclusively, I still didn't love him. I liked him. I liked kissing him and spending time with him, but I didn't love him."

Lucy opened her mouth to speak, but this time Mel continued. "He was in love with me. That's what he said, anyway."

"You didn't believe him?"

"Maybe. Oh, I don't know." Mel gave a little laugh that sounded almost like a sob. "Yes, I think he did. Or maybe he didn't. How could I know for sure? Did how he felt even matter if I didn't feel the same?"

Lucy did her best to make sense of her friend's rambling. The trouble was, she wasn't certain if Mel was trying to make sense of all this in her own mind or making some kind of point.

"When you returned to Holly Pointe, you told me the breakup was difficult." Lucy spoke carefully, feeling her way over unfamiliar terrain. "Though you didn't say it, I assumed that meant that both of you were hurt by the split."

"We were. For different reasons."

Lucy waited, sensing her friend had more to say.

"I broke his heart." Mel's lips curved downward. "I realize that now. Alex is a good man. I wish I could have loved him. I tried. I really did try."

"You can't make yourself love someone you don't."

"True." Mel met Lucy's gaze. "You also can't stop yourself from loving someone you do."

Lucy stiffened.

"Why are you telling me this, Mel? Why are you putting this on me? You know, with Kevin, we were so young. We were always thinking about the future, about what we'd do eventually. But then cancer stole our future." Lucy blew out an exasperated breath. "And, yes, since his death, I've been stuck in the past. With Trevor, I'm finally living in the present for the first time. Why can't you support that?"

Mel opened her mouth, then closed it without speaking.

"I'm sorry for how your relationship with Alex ended, but that was your relationship. It's not enough that I've been haunted by my past for five years. Now I have to be haunted by yours, too?"

"I'm sorry, Lucy." Mel's voice shook with emotion. "That's not what I meant. Of course I support you. Forget I said anything."

The slump to Mel's shoulders and the misery in her eyes tugged at Lucy's heartstrings.

"Consider it forgotten." Lucy leaned over and gave Mel a hug. "I'm sorry, too."

But long after her friend had left, Lucy couldn't stop thinking about what Mel had said about Alex. *Holding tight to what used to be isn't fair to anyone.*

Trevor's phone dinged, announcing a text, just as the last vendor left the Big Barn. It had been a busy day, but a satisfying one, Trevor thought, slipping the phone from his pocket.

He liked Austin and the other guys on the crew. Working the Marketplace had also allowed him to become acquainted with many of the vendors.

Glancing down at the screen, he saw the text was from Lucy. *My house in 30?*

He smiled as he sent the thumbs-up emoji.

After taking a quick shower in the employee lounge, Trevor headed straight for Lucy's house. His heart gave a leap when the door opened before he'd even reached the top step of her porch.

"Come inside. I have wine." When she saw him hesitate, she added, "Or some incredible hot cocoa mix from the Bean. I've even got sugar cookies."

"You don't need to sweeten the pot," he told her with a grin. "You had me at 'come inside.'"

Her laughter wrapped around him like a caress.

"I'm not sure if I said this before, but you have a nice place here." Trevor shrugged off his coat and glanced around, taking note of the comfortable furniture in shades of gray, including an accent chair in an eye-popping red, laminate flooring in gray planks and kitchen with black appliances.

"I had the interior updated about three years ago. When we bought the place, it was pretty sad inside, but it had potential. I sometimes worry I went too modern, but I think it works."

As Trevor handed her his coat and she continued to talk about the renovation, he realized it was nervous chatter.

He knew that this home held a lot of memories for her, but she was the one who'd invited him here. They could have met anywhere else.

"Is everything okay?"

She made a face. "I've been rambling, haven't I?"

Trevor hesitated. "Maybe just a little."

She laughed. "Or maybe a lot. I've just been looking forward to being alone with you all day."

Wrapping his arms around her, Trevor pulled her close, feeling the rapid beat of her heart against his chest. "I've been wanting to hold you like this all day."

"Do you want to grab the cocoa mix—it's in the cupboard to the right of the microwave—while I get out the cookies?"

"In a minute," he said. "Unless you're in a rush. I'm liking right where I am at the moment."

"I'm liking it, too." She relaxed against him, and he heard her breathing steady. "Lots more than cocoa and cookies."

He brushed a kiss against her hair and stroked her back with the tips of his fingers. "I could stand here holding you all night."

"Mel came by to see me today."

Trevor's fingers stilled for only a second. He thought of what Mel had said to him last night. Surely she wouldn't have told Lucy he loved her.

"Did she have anything interesting to say?"

Lucy's breath hitched ever so slightly.

Darn it, Trevor thought, Mel *had* told her.

"She brought up her old boyfriend. Apparently, he contacted her to wish her happy holidays, or something like that."

This was definitely not what he'd expected. "That was nice."

Lucy expelled a heavy breath. "I guess."

"Are they not on good terms?"

She hesitated so long that Trevor thought she wasn't going to answer. "Mel thinks he's still in love with her."

"Hmmm."

"She feels bad that she doesn't love him back."

"Can't make yourself love someone you don't."

"You're referring to Anna Beth."

"Who else?"

"It just made me think how hard it would be to hope your feelings are reciprocated and find out they aren't. To want something and not know if the other person wants it, too."

Putting his hands on her shoulders, Trevor held her at arm's length and searched her face. "Are you trying to tell me something, Lucy?"

"I want you to make love to me, Trevor. I need to know if you want it, too."

Lucy awakened the next morning in her own bed. Unlike all the other mornings, this time she wasn't alone.

He smiled as her lashes fluttered open.

He'd been awake for the last twenty minutes, enjoying watching her sleep. The slight rise and fall of her chest, the little smile on her lips and the way her warm body snuggled against his filled him with contentment.

He thought of the Christmas gift he was making her, and his lips curved as he imagined her response when she saw it.

"What brings that smile to your lips so early?"

Just Lucy's voice, husky with sleep, stirred something in him. Trevor knew he could no longer deny what had happened. He wasn't falling in love with Lucy, he was in love with her.

"Trevor?"

The question in her voice reminded him that he hadn't answered her.

"You bring the smile to my face. Being here with you." Trevor brushed the hair back from Lucy's sweet face with his palm and kissed her gently. "Can I make you breakfast? Or take you out?"

She stretched. "I've been meaning to get to the store, but haven't quite got that done. So, unless you have a fierce desire for a breakfast of cookies and coffee, we should probably go out."

"I should put on some clothes first."

"Naw. You look great naked." She gave her eyebrows a wiggle.

"Flatterer." He laughed and kissed her, this time letting his mouth linger on those sweet lips.

"We don't have to rush out and eat right away," she told him.

He grinned. "Exactly my thoughts."

CHAPTER SEVENTEEN

The diner's large picture windows sported decorative Christmas clings. Greenery, interspersed with lights and bows, surrounded the front entrance.

Though it was a Sunday morning, which at this time of year practically guaranteed a busy café no matter the time, Lucy decided they must have hit a lull, because she and Trevor were able to snag a booth without a wait.

"Hey, two of my favorite people." Melinda flashed a smile as she sauntered up to the booth. "What can I get you?"

Lucy smiled at her friend, glad to see the light back in Mel's eyes.

With her hair pulled back in a jaunty tail and a bright smile on red lips that matched her Rosie's Diner T-shirt, Mel appeared to have regained her Christmas cheer.

"How's your morning been so far?" Trevor asked Mel.

"Not too bad. How about you?"

When Trevor glanced at Lucy and smiled, she wondered if he was remembering their time in bed. Or maybe when they'd decided to share the shower.

"I've had a most excellent morning so far." He shifted his gaze to Mel. "In terms of what I want to eat, I haven't really taken time to look at the menu. Could you give me a few minutes?"

Mel turned to Lucy. "Don't bother pretending to look. You always get the same thing."

"You never know. I may go rogue this morning."

"I'll believe that when I see it." Mel's hand poised above the turned-over cups on the table. "Coffee?"

"Yes," Lucy and Trevor said at once, then exchanged a look and laughed.

Mel flipped over the cups and smiled. "I'll bring the pot."

The second Melinda was out of earshot, Lucy leaned forward. "A 'most excellent morning'?"

Trevor arched a brow. "Well, it was for me. From the way you were moaning, I thought it was for you as well."

"Keep your voice down." Despite the admonishment, Lucy couldn't stop the smile or the pleasure that surged when Trevor reached across the table and covered her hand with his.

She curved her fingers around his broad palm, remembering how good that rough touch had felt against her bare skin.

"You're going to have to let go of her for just a second." Mel lifted the coffeepot, the corners of her lips twitching. "Safety hazard."

"If you insist," Trevor teased, releasing Lucy's hand.

"Ready to order? If not, I can come back."

"I'm ready." Lucy spoke, then realized Trevor still hadn't looked at the menu. "But—"

"I'll have whatever she's having." Trevor closed the menu he'd had yet to peruse.

"French toast, side of bacon?" Mel winked at Lucy, then shifted her gaze to Trevor, seeking confirmation.

"Sounds good," Trevor told her.

"Thanks for making it so easy. Your food should be out in a jiffy." Mel flipped over her notepad and moved to the next table.

"We didn't talk this morning about today's plans," Trevor said.

"Of course, from what I recall, there wasn't much talking going on."

Lucy nearly spit out her coffee. Once she composed herself, she just shook her head.

Even with his hair mussed and a night's worth of stubble on his face, Trevor still made her heart go pitter-patter. "The Marketplace is going on today, but I think the crew has that under control."

"No emus named Pretty to get things stirred up?"

"Definitely no emus."

They exchanged a smile, and once again he reached across the table to take her hand. He was playing with her fingers when Melinda arrived with their food.

"Break it up, you two," she said good-naturedly, setting their plates on the table. "This is a triple-G-rated establishment."

Lucy only rolled her eyes.

Trevor bit. "What's a triple-G rating?"

"It's like G-rated, only three times as sweet and wholesome," Lucy answered before Mel had a chance. "Rosie was a real stickler about movies Mel watched when she was little. Mine? Well, I could have been watching R-rated movies at five for all Paula cared."

"Interesting." Trevor rubbed his chin. "So let me get this straight. Since this place is triple-G that means I can't hold Lucy's hand?"

"Nope, and stop with those puppy-dog looks." Mel tried for stern, but failed. "Those are off-limits, too."

"Puppy-dog looks?" Trevor asked, appearing startled.

"It's where you look at the person as if they're the one you love most in the world. Kind of like a dog does."

Lucy avoided looking at Trevor while Mel was making her explanation. When Mel was out of earshot, she glanced at Trevor and found him staring. She was trying to figure out who was looking at who with puppy-dog eyes when Derek scooted in beside Lucy.

Derek waved his sister away when she started over. "I can't stay but a minute."

"What's up?" Trevor asked.

"Zach and I were supposed to help out during sled bowling at Dobson's Hill this afternoon, but we got a call from Jan and Almira Perrin that their garage roof collapsed. They want someone out there ASAP. Almira's car is in the garage. We need to get her car out and repair the roof."

"Are they okay?" Concern furrowed Lucy's brows. "How badly was their house damaged?"

"It wasn't the garage attached to the house. This one was old and already on the verge of collapse when she and Jan bought the acreage. We gave her a bid a couple of years ago to fix the roof, but they didn't want to spend the money." Derek fixed his gaze on Trevor. "I tried reaching out to Sam. He's the event coordinator, but I got his voice mail. Sled bowling is a big hit with the kids. We've got some teenage volunteers—Camryn being one— but someone needs to supervise them setting up the bowling pins and—"

"Bowling pins?" Trevor's question stopped Derek's ramblings.

"They're red and green and super cute," Lucy answered, then turned to Derek. "What time do you need us there?"

The way Lucy explained it to Trevor, the purpose of sled bowling was to ride a sled down Dobson's Hill and knock down as many of the pins set up at the bottom as possible.

There was a nominal fee to enter with all sorts of prizes being offered. That fact, as well as the day being sunny and in the lower thirties, brought the kids out in droves.

After a short discussion on the way over—and after speaking

with Sam and getting his blessing—they decided that Lucy would oversee top-of-the-hill stuff, and Trevor would be the bottom-of-the-hill coordinator.

Lucy's "staff" of teens, including Derek's daughter, would check in the entrants, assign them a number and collect their fee.

If Lucy's staff was the brains of the operation, Trevor decided his "staff" was the brawn. They would set up the bowling pins, count the number of pins knocked down and record that info next to the entry number of the sled.

Each entrant went down the hill three times. Once everyone who'd entered had completed three runs, tallies would be done. Since only the top three received big prizes, there would be a runoff among the top entrants.

Because of the number of participants, there was a lot of setting up of pins and a lot of coordination needed. Especially with three "alleys" for the sleds to go down.

Trevor liked the kids he worked with. They had a job to do, and they did it without grousing, other than some good-natured PG-rated trash talk.

Stella was there, taking pictures for the town's website and other media pages. Sam arrived later with his parents in tow.

The older couple didn't just stand around and watch, like many of the parents who'd come to cheer on their kids, they pitched in to help.

Though he didn't know him well, Trevor liked that Geoff wasn't afraid to get his hands dirty.

Only when the three sleds that were vying for first, second and third sat at the top of the hill did Geoff slap Trevor on the back. "I'm going to find my wife."

"Thanks for the help, Geoff." Trevor cast a quick glance at the bottom of the hill, where three sets of bowling pins were set up and ready. He gave a thumbs-up to his teenage crew. "We needed it."

"I understand from Sam that you and Lucy got called to fill in at the last minute."

"We were having breakfast at Rosie's when Derek came in and told us that he and Zach were needed on an emergency job." Trevor smiled at the sight of Lucy appearing to deliver a pep talk to the three finalists at the top of the hill. "She's amazing."

Trevor wasn't aware he'd spoken the words aloud until Geoff responded.

"Lucy is a special woman. She deserves only the best." Geoff met Trevor's gaze. "See that you don't disappoint her."

~

"Trevor and I will make sure that the pins get put away," Lucy told the teens once the event concluded.

She'd come down off the mountain for the ceremony when the final three were given their prizes by Bonnie Spomer, owner of the Back Porch restaurant, who was dressed like a reindeer.

"You sure?" A boy Trevor recognized as Brick, one of Kenny and Norma's grandkids, hesitated. "Me and my friends can stay and help clean up."

"If we do, we'll miss playing pond hockey." His friend's voice stopped just short of a whine. "They're choosing teams at three."

"Well, if you're sure it's okay..." Brick shifted from one foot to the other, no longer appearing so eager to stay.

"Positive." Trevor gestured with his head toward Lucy. "Ms. Cummings and I have it under control."

"Cool." The boys hurried to join their friends. Then, like a pack of young wolves, they took off at a fast trot.

"Surely they're not going to run all the way to the pond," Trevor said as they disappeared from view.

"There are tons of people headed to the pond. They won't have any trouble catching a ride. That's why the hill cleared out so quickly. Dustin is doing some kind of clinic right before the kids' game. No one wants to miss that."

Trevor should have realized this wasn't the only activity going on in Holly Pointe this weekend. December in this town was nonstop activities.

He glanced at the deserted hill. "The hockey game at the pond still doesn't explain why the hill is so empty."

Lucy gave a little laugh. She wore a blue ski cap today that matched the sky and her eyes, and her cheeks and lips were red from the cold. "There are signs all over indicating that the hill is closed until four for the sledding competition."

That explained it, Trevor thought. "Since every entrant got a prize, I asked one of the kids if he knew what the prize was. You know what he told me?"

"A snow cone."

"How did you know that?" Trevor shook his head. "And why a snow cone?"

"They can get either a snow cone or a candy cone. It's the same prize every year. I honestly think we'd have a revolt if it changed."

"When I was a kid, I'd probably have liked it, too."

"I haven't been a kid for quite a while, but I still love snow cones." Lucy's lips curved. "Clyde's has a cherry pie candy cone that's to die for."

"Clyde's?"

"Clyde's Candy Cones. He started the business about ten years ago. The coupon allows them to pick from all different flavors of snow cones, or they can choose a small candy cone."

"What exactly is a candy cone?"

"They're cups filled with ice cream topped with snow and whipped cream, some topping—cherry is my fav—and more whipped cream."

"That sounds really good." He offered a smile. "Want to get one now?"

Lucy's eyes slid up the hill. "I have something better in mind."

~

"I can't believe you had two sleds in your trunk." Trevor sat on top of the inflatable blue toboggan, while Lucy resided on a red one.

"Like I told you last night," Lucy shot him an impish smile, "I believe in being prepared."

Trevor eyed the pins at the bottom of the hill that suddenly seemed so far away.

"Are you ready?" she asked, the question breaking into his thoughts.

"As I'll ever be."

"Three, two, one, go."

He pushed off and flew down the hill, the trees on either side of the hill whizzing by at breathtaking speed. It had been years since he'd been on a sled, and never on one that had gone this fast.

"Whoo-eee," he called out, caught up in the joy of the moment.

To his right, he saw Lucy's red sled rush past him. He had to remind himself that this wasn't a race. It didn't matter who reached the bottom first—what mattered was how many pins they each knocked down.

Though Lucy made an enchanting sight with her blonde hair flying from beneath her stocking cap, Trevor told himself to concentrate on the pins.

The pins were in sight, and utilizing a technique learned from his time spent today at the bottom of the hill, he spun his sled sideways.

The kids he'd watched do it had sworn you could knock down more pins with your sled hitting them sideways than you could hitting them straight on with your feet.

"Strike," he yelled when his body and sled sent all the pins flying.

The pins slowed his momentum, but it was the tiny bump of snow that he hit that had him careening sideways into Lucy.

They tumbled off their sleds and rolled in the snow with Lucy ending up on top.

His first thought when he heard the sound she was making was that he'd hurt her. "Omigod, Lucy, I'm so sorry."

Only when he looked up into her twinkling blue eyes did he realize she wasn't crying, she was laughing.

"That was a blast." Bending down, she pressed her ice-cold lips to his. "Let's do it again. Only this time, let's go down together."

It took him a few seconds to process that idea.

By then, she was a good distance up the hill, dragging her red sled behind her.

He quickly caught up to her. "How many pins did you knock down?"

Her brows pulled together in a little frown. "I'm not sure. Right after I hit the pins, you hit me, and then we both hit the pins. They were all on the ground, but I'm not sure if I knocked them down or if you did."

"It was a joint effort." He took her free hand and raised it high. "We won."

She looked at him for a long moment. "I believe we have."

CHAPTER EIGHTEEN

The next week sped by so quickly that Trevor felt at times that he would blink and the month would be over. He wished everything would just slow down.

Trevor worked on his carvings during the day, unless Hedy or Lucy or some event in Holly Pointe beckoned, and he spent every evening with Lucy.

His Christmas gift for her had begun to take shape. Initially, he'd planned for it to be simply her face carved into a piece of wood, but he thought—hoped—she'd like this incarnation even more.

On Friday, Trevor showed up at the Baby Barn at three. Though the wedding tonight wasn't until six, he'd come early to help Lucy set up the chairs. He now considered himself to be an expert.

Normally, the couple would have hired a DOC to do the setup, but Lucy had confided that this couple was paying for the wedding themselves and had spent nearly their entire wedding budget on the venue.

"Couldn't you give them a break on the rental of the Barn?" Trevor asked, arranging another one of the wooden chairs. No fancy chair covering or bows on these. Still, in his estimation, the white lacquered chairs looked great the way they were.

"I don't do special deals." Lucy's tone was matter-of-fact. "Running an operation of this size is expensive, and I need the revenue. Each time I'm tempted to give a discount, I have to tell myself that it isn't fair to those who've paid full price. Most people don't mention their financial circumstances, so maybe it's a hardship for them."

"I understand."

"The bottom line is, there are any number of places where this couple could be married that would cost them far less money. If they want to get married here, they pay the going rate."

Trevor nodded, sensing he'd hit a hot button. The thing was, he did understand. He was often approached by people who wanted a discount on his art. For all the reasons Lucy had mentioned, the answer was no more often than yes.

As he set down another chair, his gaze was drawn to the front of the church and the beautiful floral arrangements. He gestured with one hand. "If money is tight, how did they afford those flowers?"

Lucy smiled. "Those were from a wedding this morning. That couple was from out of state, and the entire bridal party and family were staying at Jay Peak Resort. They had no place to put them and no desire to do anything with the flowers. I called tonight's bride, and she was thrilled to have them. Other than her bridal bouquet, they'd decided to go without flowers."

"They scored big with these."

"Yes, they did."

"Have you ever thought of what kind of wedding you'd like?"

"Pardon?"

"What's your dream wedding?" Trevor glanced around. "You've likely seen all kinds of weddings here and more that you've attended through the years."

"I guess I've never thought about it."

"Oh c'mon. You and Kevin were together all those years. Surely you discussed the type of wedding you'd both like." The second the comment left his lips, Trevor wished he'd kept his mouth shut.

He'd been curious, that's all, but realized now that he didn't want to imagine Lucy planning her wedding to another man. If she was thinking of a wedding, of walking down the aisle toward a man who looked at her with love in his eyes, he wanted her to be envisioning him.

"I never did come up with a plan for a wedding when Kevin and I were together."

Instead of letting it be and moving on to another subject, he had to ask, "Why not?"

"I don't know why." She appeared so befuddled he knew she was being honest. "Maybe because I was so young, and marriage seemed far away. Or maybe my mom jumping in and out of marriages had something to do with my hesitation. I loved Kevin, but marriage was not something I desired right then. Then he got sick and—"

"There you are. I've been looking all over for you."

Trevor turned and saw his dream of a quiet night with Lucy go down the drain as a beautiful woman in her late forties with a mass of blonde hair strode down the aisle in three-inch heels.

After casting a curious glance at Trevor, the woman held out her hands to Lucy. "Come and give your mother a hug."

Lucy set down the chair she was holding and dutifully did as her mother said. The scent of jasmine, too liberally applied, surrounded her, and she fought hard not to sneeze.

The old adage *a little goes a long way* applied to this wonderful fragrance that Paula considered her signature scent.

Stepping back from the brief embrace, Lucy eyed her mother.

"This is a surprise. I thought you liked mojitos and palm trees at Christmas."

Paula laughed as if she'd made a joke. "I planned to spend Christmas in South Beach this year, but Carlos and I hit the skids a few days ago." She heaved a melodramatic sigh. "He'd rented the condo under his own name, which left me with no decent place to stay."

"Breaking up with you just before the holidays wasn't very nice of him," Lucy said in a droll tone. "Not to mention terribly inconvenient."

"I broke up with him, dear daughter." Paula waved a dismissive hand. "Good riddance to bad rubbish."

"Well, it's nice to see you." Lucy pointed to the stacks of chairs. "I'd love to chat, but as you can see, there's still work to be done."

Paula sniffed. "I don't know why you don't have hired help do this. Why you insist on doing manual labor is beyond me."

Had her mother really forgotten what it was like to struggle? Paula hadn't grown up in luxury, far from it. When she'd married husband number one, Lucy's father, she'd been seventeen and pregnant.

He had worked hard, but Paula hadn't been content to live paycheck to paycheck. Lucy hadn't even been a year old when they'd divorced. He'd left the area and started a new life in another state.

Paula had chosen more carefully with each successive marriage. Money had become more important to her than looks, although she did appreciate a good-looking man.

Paula's gaze turned calculating as she shifted her focus to Trevor. She strode across the highly polished wood flooring toward him, all smiles.

"I don't believe we've met."

"It's been a long time." Trevor offered a friendly smile. "I'm Trevor Sherwood, Angie's son."

Paula's eyes widened. For a second, her lips, covered in a bright pink, formed a perfect O.

"You're little Trevor?" Paula gave an incredulous laugh. "I never would have believed it. I guess I haven't seen you in a while."

"Not since my mom married Chad."

"Don't mention that man's name to me." Paula lifted her hands. "I know he's your stepfather, but any man that would keep a woman from her best friend, well, he's not a man I like."

"I don't know about him keeping her from you, but I do agree with you on his character."

A spark flickered in Paula's eyes. "You don't like him either."

"Not particularly."

"Well, well." Paula looped her arm through Trevor's. "It appears we have something in common. I have to say I knew I liked you the moment I set eyes on you. Why don't you and I go somewhere quiet, and you can catch me up on what's going on with my dear friend Angie and that horrible Chad?"

"I wouldn't be any help in terms of updates." Trevor's tone remained matter-of-fact as he disentangled Paula's hand from his arm. "Plus, I can't leave. I promised my grandmother I'd help Lucy through the holidays, or until she hires a new assistant."

Lucy hadn't told her mother about Hedy's retirement. Her mother might own the Barns, but Lucy handled everything to do with operations.

The wheels began turning in her mother's head, and Lucy could see Paula putting the pieces together. Her mother wasn't just a pretty face with a figure that Lucy envied, she was smart. A stupid woman, no matter how pretty, didn't attract the caliber of men she'd married the last couple of times.

"What happened to your grandmother?" Paula directed the question to Trevor.

That, too, was to be expected. Her mother much preferred to interact with men.

"She decided to retire this fall." Trevor glanced at Lucy, and she gave a little nod. "Lucy's been slammed. Since I'm back in Holly Pointe over the holidays, I offered to help."

Paula's gaze shifted from him to Lucy, then back to Trevor. Her gaze turned speculative.

Lucy knew exactly how her mother's mind worked, so she wasn't surprised by the next question. "What exactly do you do for a living, Trevor? I mean, there aren't many jobs that allow a man to simply take a couple months off to see his old granny."

Trevor laughed. "I don't think Hedy would appreciate being called an old granny."

Paula didn't even flash a smile. She'd asked a question, an important question, and hadn't yet received an answer.

"What is it you do for a living?" she repeated.

"I work for myself." Trevor moved to where the chairs were stacked, picked one up and set it in place.

He was playing with her, making her work for the information, Lucy thought, unable to stop her smile.

"Doing?" Paula prompted.

"A little woodcarving." Trevor's tone was offhand. "It started out as a hobby."

Lucy had to hide a grin at the way he downplayed his talent. She'd looked up his art online and had been amazed by not only his talent, but awed by the price tags.

"Interesting," Paula said, but her tone said he was no longer of any interest to her.

"We really need to get this done," Lucy told her mother, gesturing to all the chairs still needing to be set up.

"I'll take my bag and go upstairs to freshen up while you finish here." Paula's tone had turned bored. "Once you're done, you and I will go out for dinner."

It was often said that in a conversation, people focused on the most important part. It was the bag part that had Lucy's breath catching in her throat. She forced herself to breathe, even somehow managed a smile. "Where exactly are you planning on staying while you're here?"

"Well, with you, my darling. Where else would I stay?"

"What about the apartment?" Lucy gestured with one hand.

Paula made a face. "Too small and not at all acceptable. While I'm in town, I'll be staying with you."

~

Lucy hadn't wanted to drive to Jay Peak for dinner, but her mother had insisted, claiming she'd eaten at all the cafés in Holly Pointe. When Lucy had mentioned the newly opened Jingle Shells, Paula had turned up her nose.

Choosing to dine in the nearby town of Jay Peak was one thing, but Lucy's Spidey senses sprang into overdrive when her mother insisted on driving separately.

Lucy didn't argue. The trip to Jay Peak, a short twenty-minute drive from Holly Pointe, would undoubtedly be more pleasurable alone than with her mother anyway.

At her mother's insistence, Lucy had dressed up. She'd topped a black pencil skirt with a black peplum top, then twisted her hair into a messy knot. Red heels not only added a nice pop of color, but were a necessity. It could be sleeting outside, and her mother would still insist they both wear fashionable footwear.

Before leaving, Lucy had made sure her staff had everything under control and reiterated that if they had any questions or ran into any problems, she wanted to be called.

"How did you hear of this place?" Lucy asked her mother when they were seated in the main dining room of The Grill.

"A friend," was Paula's only response.

The place had what Lucy thought of as a Vermont vibe, with a bubbling brook—now iced over—visible through the window, exposed rafters and an eclectic menu that had an odd emphasis on Asian fusion food.

Lucy ordered the Peking duck wraps and Paula the ahi tuna.

About halfway through their meal, after taking a bolstering sip of wine—another necessity when dining with her mom—Lucy broached the subject of the sale of the Barns.

Even though she was on target to be able to come up with the ten percent the bank required, one small hiccup in December and she could fall short.

"The last time we spoke about the sale of the Barns, you insisted on having the money by the end of January." Lucy absently twirled the stem of her wineglass back and forth between her fingers. "I'm on target to have the money then, but I was just wondering if, say, something happened, and it ended up being February—"

"The deadline is January thirty-first." Paula fixed a steely-eyed stare on the stem of Lucy's glass.

Lucy's fingers froze.

"As I already mentioned, I have another buyer in the wings. Very motivated." Her mother smiled brightly at the handsome waiter, who was young enough to be her son.

"How is everything?" he asked, focusing his charm on Paula, obviously deciding she would be the one leaving the tip.

"Adequate." Paula offered him a faux smile, then waved a hand in dismissal.

"You've mentioned this buyer before. Who is it?"

Paula sipped her wine before answering. "Who is not important. What's important is that they have the money and are ready to sign on the dotted line. You should be grateful I'm still giving you until the thirty-first."

Lucy bit her tongue to keep from telling her mother exactly what she thought of that "grateful" comment. Instead, she kept her mind focused on what was important—the Barns and this other potential buyer. "Are they from the area? If not, they won't know the community like I do. They'll have no knowledge of local vendors and what they need. Not to mention what our clients and customers expect."

"You say that as if it's a bad thing." Paula's gaze turned shrewd. "From a business standpoint, it will likely be an advantage. You've never understood what it takes to make money."

"You've never understood my love of Holly Pointe." Lucy couldn't quite keep the accusation from her voice.

"What I didn't understand, and never will, was why you didn't marry Kevin Johnson when you had the chance." Disapproval flickered in Paula's artfully made-up blue eyes. "His family has millions."

"That was their money, not Kevin's." They'd had this discussion before, and it didn't sit any better the second—or was it the tenth?—time around.

"Parents like his would have a bundle in life insurance on their son." Paula shook her head, giving the equivalent of a *tsk-tsk*. "How many times did I urge you to marry the guy and get him to list you as the beneficiary on those policies? If you'd done as I urged, you wouldn't be worried about money now. You'd be rolling in it."

"You urging me to do something so despicable was precisely one of the reasons I didn't marry Kevin before he died." Lucy blinked back sudden tears. "He would have willingly put me on those policies, but I didn't want his money. I wanted him."

"So instead, you refused to grant the man you loved his dying request, which we both know was to marry you, because you were stubborn and wanted to spite me." Paula gave a little laugh. "Now you're consorting with a man who carves wood for a living and expecting me to do you favors so you can have my business. Unbelievable."

Anger coursed through Lucy's veins. She couldn't recall ever being quite so angry with her mother.

"You can use the apartment or find somewhere else to stay

while you're in Holly Pointe." Lucy didn't even attempt to soften the cold edge to her tone. "I'm not opening my home to you."

"Neither your tiny, little home or that shoebox of an apartment is up to my standards anyway." Paula's expression suddenly changed. Her face lit up, and she waved. "Which is why, when I heard from an old friend that he was in the area on business, I put my bag in my car. I'll be staying here in Jay Peak with him. When he returns to Boca, I plan to go with him."

Lucy slid back her chair and pushed to her feet. She didn't care to be introduced to her mother's friend as what, her sister?

The truth was she didn't want to spend one more second in her mother's company.

Tossing a few bills on the table, she strode past the distinguished-looking man with the thick head of gray hair and wearing an expensive suit.

She wasn't even out of the building when she pulled out her phone and texted Trevor.

CHAPTER NINETEEN

Instead of spending the evening with Lucy, Trevor found himself at the Thirsty Moose with Derek and Zach.

"What's Camryn doing this evening?" Trevor asked. Derek's kid wasn't a baby, but she was young enough that someone should probably be home with her.

"She's spending the night with her friend Mia." Derek took a sip of beer. "Mia's folks are older and don't go out much."

Zach pointed the top of his beer bottle at Derek. "All the parents are older than you. Not many have a kid at seventeen."

"Lucy's mother did." Trevor scooped up a handful of bar mix.

"I wondered how long it'd take for you to mention her." Zach made a great show of pushing back the sleeve of his flannel shirt to look at his watch. "Thirty-five minutes."

"Is that a new record?" Derek asked with a straight face.

"Ha-ha." Trevor washed the last of the mix down with a swig of beer. Instead of engaging with Zach, which Trevor figured would only encourage the guy, he scanned the bar.

Nearly every table was full, most of the patrons in their twenties and thirties. Not a lot of couples, though there were a few.

Mostly tables of women eyeing the men and men checking out the women.

Unlike HJ's or Blitzen's, this bar appeared to cater to the young, single crowd. The music came from a surprisingly good rock band in one corner, and two pool tables and several dartboards were in an adjacent room.

Trevor had found Zach and Derek at a table that offered a good view of a televised ball game on mute. The table was also, Trevor had noted, not far from several tables full of women.

"So," Derek said in a casual tone that Trevor guessed was anything but casual, "how are you and Lucy getting along?"

Trevor had never been one to kiss and tell, but Derek hadn't asked if he'd slept with Lucy, only how they were getting along.

"It's going good. I enjoy spending time with her." Trevor discovered simply saying her name made him smile…and wonder how her evening with her mother was going.

When her mother had gone upstairs, Lucy had told him they'd have to reschedule their night out.

He understood.

On his way out the door, he'd called Derek.

"Are you and Lucy—?"

Derek didn't get a chance to finish his question because Trevor spotted a familiar redhead as she walked through the door. He lifted his hand, calling out, "Melinda, over here."

Mel smiled and waved. As Derek's sister wove her way to their table, Trevor saw Kate was with her.

"Hey, guys." Mel's gaze swept the table. "Where's Lucy?"

"Her mom is in town and—"

"Paula is in Holly Pointe?" Melinda's rising voice reflected her surprise. "Lucy wasn't expecting her."

"Why are you looking at him for confirmation?" Derek teased. "Aren't you and Kate supposed to be her besties?"

"Lately, Trevor has been spending more time with Lucy than

we have," Kate answered before Mel could, then fixed her green eyes on him.

"She had no idea her mother was coming." Questions answered, Trevor thought, and shifted his gaze to the television.

"You two want to sit with us?" Derek asked. "I can pull up a couple of chairs."

Kate glanced around the bar. "The place is packed."

"There are two empty seats at the bar," Mel told her, "but they aren't together."

"Sure." Kate shrugged. "We'll join you."

Trevor helped Derek retrieve two chairs that had been pushed against one wall. Once the two women were seated, he sipped his beer and listened as Kate and Mel explained how their day had gone so far.

"The café was swamped." Mel caught the eye of the server, pointed to Derek's beer and held up two fingers. "When Kate called to see if I wanted to go out, I was ser-i-ous-ly tempted to put on my pj's, order a pizza and binge a series on Netflix."

"I told Mel she's never going to meet any men while sitting at home alone," Kate said pointedly, then took the beer Mel offered that the female server had just dropped off.

"Yes, and look how well that worked out." Mel took a long drink from the bottle.

Kate inclined her head.

"Think about it." Melinda pointed to Derek. "Who are we going to meet sitting at a table with my brother?"

Kate laughed. "Good point."

"Thinking only of yourself." Zach heaved out an exaggerated breath. "Who are we going to meet with women already with us?"

Trevor's phone dinged. Pulling it out, he saw a text from Lucy.

Where R U? Want company?
Thirsty Moose. Yes.
Give me 30.

Trevor gave the comment a thumbs-up emoji and pocketed his phone.

Mel slanted a curious glance in his direction, but didn't ask.

Trevor glanced around the bar and spotted an unused chair at a table close to the door. He pushed to his feet. "Be right back."

As Trevor pushed the chair between him and Kate, he said, "Lucy's going to be joining us."

"I thought she was with her mom tonight," Mel said.

Trevor shrugged. He relaxed against the back of his chair. While he hoped things hadn't gone south with Paula, he was happy that Lucy had contacted him.

Soon, she would be sitting beside him.

The night was about to get much better.

The dress code at the Thirsty Moose ran to jeans with flannel shirts or sweaters. In her skirt and heels, Lucy knew she stood out like Santa at a princess convention. As she scanned the crowded bar for Trevor, she realized she didn't care.

When her eyes met his, it struck her that he'd been watching the door.

Watching for me.

She lifted a hand in acknowledgment, then started making her way to where he sat. Every table in the place was filled, many with extra chairs shoved around the small tabletops.

Some of the people she knew, and she greeted them with a smile or a quick hello. She ignored the admiring glances from various men in the crowd, as well as the occasional, "Hey, sweetheart, you can sit with me."

Lucy might have told those guys she wasn't anyone's sweetheart, but that might not have been entirely accurate. Not with Trevor moving through the crowded tables to greet her. After the misadventures she'd had with her mother, his warm welcoming smile brought tears to her eyes.

"Hey," he said when he reached her. "I'm glad you texted."

"I'm glad your evening was still open."

"It's always open for you."

She didn't know how he managed it, but when he took her hand and led her to the table, a wide path seemed to open before her. Or maybe the feel of her hand in his simply had her relaxing.

When he'd texted back that he was at the Thirsty Moose, Lucy had assumed he was with a couple of guys. She hadn't expected to see her friends.

"Mel. Kate." Lucy took a seat in the chair Trevor pulled out, reluctantly letting go of his hand. "This is a nice surprise."

"For us, too." Mel's gaze turned assessing. "I didn't expect to see you this evening. Trevor mentioned something about you being out for dinner with your mother."

It might have been a statement, but Lucy heard the question. She was struggling with how to answer. The incident with her mother had unnerved her, and she still felt unsettled.

Then, beneath the table, Trevor took her hand, linking their fingers together. It was such a small gesture, but one that meant the world to her.

"My mom wanted to check out The Grill in Jay Peak."

"I take it Rosie's wasn't good enough for her," Mel joked.

Lucy fluttered her free hand in the air. "She picked the place, not me. I had the Peking duck wraps, which were pretty tasty."

"I haven't been to that restaurant." Kate took a sip of beer. "But I've heard good things."

"It's pretty inside, with some unique options on the menu. I think you'd like it." Thankful that it was her left hand that Trevor held, Lucy picked up his bottle of beer with a questioning glance. At his answering nod, she took a sip.

"Is that why your mom wanted to go there?" Mel asked. "There's certainly no Peking duck wraps on Rosie's menu."

"I thought that at first." Though the man her mother had been meeting wasn't really a part of the story, he'd shown up shortly after their discussion, and Lucy couldn't help but consider him part of it all. Consequently, her voice trembled ever so slightly until she brought it under control. "It was a man."

Beneath the table, Trevor's thumb began to slowly massage her palm.

Instead of arousing her, as it might have at another time, the gesture soothed, comforted and steadied her.

"Who was he?" Derek asked, speaking for the first time. "Anyone we know?"

"No. At least I'd never seen him before." Lucy took another sip of Trevor's beer and found it suited her more than the expensive wine she'd consumed earlier. She slanted a glance at Trevor. "She's planning to stay with him at the resort, then fly out with him when he leaves for Florida."

"Why did she even come to Holly Pointe?" Kate's brows pulled together in confusion. "Trevor said she just got into town this afternoon."

When her gaze shifted to Trevor, he met her questioning one with a steady one of his own. "All I said when they asked about you was that your mother showed up at the Barns this afternoon, and we weren't together because you'd gone out for dinner with her."

Lucy got the message: Trevor wanted to make it clear he hadn't been sitting around gossiping about her this evening.

"All true." Lucy resisted the urge to sigh. "I have no clue why she showed up, unless it was because she knew this guy was at Jay Peak and wanted to be able to tell him she'd been visiting family in Holly Pointe."

"Would she really do that?" Zach asked.

The others at the table, more familiar with Paula's machinations than Zach, laughed.

Enough talk about her wonderful mother, Lucy thought.

"So you all decided to go out together this evening?" she asked Trevor.

"I met Zach and Derek here," Trevor said.

"And Mel and I crashed the party," Kate explained. "Or rather, the guys had a table, and the others were full."

"Sitting with your brother isn't ideal when you want to scope out the available men." Mel's eyes brightened, and she popped up so quickly she reminded Lucy of a jack-in-the-box. "A two-top just opened up near the band."

"I'll grab it." Kate was already sprinting toward it when Mel turned to Lucy. "We could pull up a chair, and you could join us." Then Mel focused on Trevor. "I'd invite you, but it's a girls-only table."

Trevor chuckled, but his gaze shifted to Lucy. *Whatever you want to do,* the look seemed to say.

"We had plans for the evening." Lucy never took her gaze off his. "If you're still—"

"I am."

Lucy smiled at Mel. "I appreciate the offer, but—"

"Thanks, but no, thanks." Mel shot her an impish smile. "That's okay. A manhunt is no fun when you already have a man."

Once Mel left, Lucy met Trevor's gaze. "Are you ready to go? Or do you want to stay longer?"

In answer, Trevor pushed to his feet, still holding her hand. "Let's go."

Lucy wasn't sure where they were going. Frankly, it didn't matter.

All that mattered was she was with Trevor, and she could finally breathe normally again.

CHAPTER TWENTY

"Where should I meet you?" Trevor slanted a glance at Lucy when they reached her car.

Since they'd both driven, they were faced with one car too many.

"Why don't you come to my place? I can change out of this skirt and heels, and we'll decide where to go from there."

"I like the heels."

She smiled. "So do I, but it's been a long day. I'm ready to kick back and relax."

"Will your mother and her friend be stopping by?"

"She's not coming back to Holly Pointe. Personally, I don't think she ever planned to stay." Lucy gave a little laugh. "I thought it strange that she insisted on driving separately to Jay Peak for dinner and had her bag in the car."

"So she—"

Lucy's hand on his arm stopped him. "I'll tell you all about it when we get to my house."

He bent over and covered her mouth with his. "See you there."

The drive didn't take long. Once inside Lucy's house and seated on the comfortable sofa with the furnace flooding the room with warmth, he realized Lucy had been right. This was a much better place for a conversation than a parking lot.

It didn't take Lucy long to change her clothes. She came out of the bedroom in leggings and a blue sweater. Though he knew she liked to dress up, it looked as if simply changing—or maybe it was her mother being gone—had removed ten pounds of weight from her shoulders.

Trevor pushed to his feet when she entered the living room. "You look lots more chill."

She motioned him back down, then dropped down on the sofa beside him. "The worst of the night is behind me."

"At least the food was good."

Lucy tossed back her head and laughed. "There you go looking on the bright side again."

With a finger, Trevor slipped a stray strand of hair back behind her ear. "Anything to bring that smile back."

Lucy expelled an audible breath and rested her head against his shoulder. "I could lose the Barns."

Trevor stilled. "What happened?"

"My mother is going to hold me to the January thirty-first date to secure the financing and close on the loan."

He slowly ran a hand up her arm in a gesture intended to soothe. "I'm confused. Hasn't that been the deadline all along?"

Lucy nodded. "I just keep thinking if one thing goes wrong…"

"Why are you worried about it now?"

"I think it's because it's getting close, and I want it so much," Lucy admitted. "I asked my mother tonight if she'd consider an extension into February, just in case I can't meet the January deadline."

"Let me guess. The answer was no."

"Not only no, but she reminded me she has a person eager to buy the Barns if the sale to me falls through." Lucy blew out a breath. "I could understand it if she needed the money for something urgent, but she doesn't."

After a long moment, which had Lucy once again leaning back and Trevor settling his arm around her shoulders, he finally spoke. "I'm sorry about this, Luce. I don't think it's right, and I really don't like her disappointing you again."

"Do you know she told me I wouldn't be in this predicament if I'd married Kevin?"

Trevor puzzled over that remark for several seconds. "I don't understand."

"According to her, if I'd married Kevin, I could have gotten him to add me as the beneficiary on his life insurance policies. I could have collected big on his death."

Trevor winced. The problem was he could imagine Paula saying those words. Heck, he could imagine his mother agreeing with her.

"I think…" Lucy spoke in a tone so low he had to strain to hear her. "I think that was part of the reason I didn't marry him."

Trevor's attempt to wrap his head around that logic came up short. "Replay that one for me."

"Kevin's family does have a lot of money. Initially, I put off getting married, not because I didn't love him, but because we were happy together the way we were. At that time, simply being with him was enough for me."

Trevor gave her shoulder a supportive squeeze and offered an encouraging smile.

"I've read about couples who marry when they learn one of them is dying, and I think that's wonderful if that's what feels right to them. Doing that wouldn't have felt right to me."

"I'm sure Kevin knew you loved him. That's what mattered."

Lucy nodded, and her eyes took on a distant glow. "Kevin loved the Mistletoe Ball. I wish I hadn't had to cancel it this year. The ball brings our community together in a way that nothing else does. Will the other potential buyer realize that? Will they even care?"

"Hard to say."

"I'll tell you one thing." Lucy ran a hand through her hair. "When I buy the Barns, I'm putting the ball back on the schedule. That's a promise."

~

The last full week before Christmas was a busy one for Lucy. Three holiday parties in the Baby Barns boosted revenue. This evening, the vendors in the Marketplace would begin tearing down their booths. This would give Lucy and her staff plenty of time to set up for the large wedding and reception on Friday.

The money the wedding would bring in, plus the corporate event on Saturday and Sunday, would give her the money she needed.

She was cutting it close, but everything was falling into place.

"The snow is picking up." Austin stuck his head into her office.

Lucy gave a little laugh. "It's December in Vermont. What else is new?"

"No, I mean it's really coming down." Austin gestured to her office window. She kept the blinds drawn because the window opened to an outdoor walkway. "See for yourself. Some of the vendors are packing up early."

Frowning, Lucy pushed back her chair and stood. Vendors never left early. She crossed the short distance to the window and flicked open the blinds. Tiny flakes fell as if they'd been dumped from a barrel in the sky.

"Have you heard the forecast?" she asked.

"Which one?" Austin rolled his eyes. "They've revised it two or three times since I got here at six."

Not a good sign, Lucy thought, considering it was only noon. "You've alerted the maintenance staff to keep the lots and walkways clear?"

"Yes, ma'am."

Lucy flinched. When had she become a ma'am? She shoved the disturbing thought aside. "Thanks for letting me know, Austin. I'm going to check and make sure everything is in place for the wedding on Friday. Then I'll be out on the floor. My phone will be with me in case you need to reach me."

"Gotcha." Austin gave a nod and disappeared down the hall.

After making a quick call to Kinsley and confirming all was in place for Friday's event, Lucy made her way to the Marketplace.

Austin had been right, she thought, but there weren't simply one or two vendors closing up early. She'd venture to say the majority were taking down their displays.

She told herself it didn't matter if they left early. They'd already paid for their booth space. Though she hated the thought of their products not being available to those who wanted to do a little more Christmas shopping.

Unfortunately, one of the vendors she wouldn't mind leaving early was still there. Mitch sat on a stool in his booth, slurping down coffee. When he saw Lucy, he set down his cup and pushed to his feet.

"If I don't see you before, you and Doreen have a good Christmas," she said.

Without giving him a chance to respond, Lucy turned and strode quickly down the aisle, not stopping until she was far, far away from Mitch and his gloom.

She turned the corner and ran into Austin. "Fancy meeting you here."

Not only didn't he return her smile, the harried look on his face had her worry-meter skyrocketing.

"What's wrong?" Taking him by the arm, she pulled him out of earshot of the vendors.

"They've closed all the airports in the region."

Lucy blew out a breath. The weather had to be bad for such closures. People who lived in Vermont were used to heavy snow. "What's the most recent revised forecast?"

"The snow is falling at a rate of two inches an hour."

"Two?" Lucy's voice rose and cracked. "How long do they expect that to continue?"

"One of the forecasters said we could get thirty-five inches."

Lucy blinked.

"He said the record is thirty-four inches, set in 2010."

"Nearly three feet of snow." Lucy forced herself to breathe. "We'll be okay, though. "All the snowplows will be mobilizing," she said, almost to herself. "They'll keep the roads open. Within twenty-four hours, everything will be clear."

"If it's still falling tomorrow, everything might not be cleared until Friday."

The couple getting married on Friday were from Bennington, nearly four hours away in the southern portion of the state.

The family and the bridal party were scheduled to arrive tomorrow, with most of their guests likely driving up the day of the ceremony.

"Even if the forecasters are right, the couple and their family should still be able to make it in on Friday," Lucy reassured herself. "I'm going to call and let them know that we'll do whatever we can to accommodate them, other than changing the date. With the corporate event beginning on Saturday, our hands are tied."

"What if the snow continues, and neither the wedding nor the corporate event happens?"

Lucy gave a humorless chuckle. "If that happens, then my worst fears will have come true."

Trevor spent most of Wednesday working on Lucy's Christmas gift. He stopped to make lunch for himself, as Hedy was busy at the Candy Cane Christmas House.

He texted Lucy a couple of times, but received only the

briefest of replies. Trevor wasn't worried. The upcoming wedding was likely consuming most of her time. He'd offered to help her prepare, but both she and Austin had insisted they had everything under control.

The snow finally stopped Thursday afternoon, falling far short of the thirty-five inches predicted. Still, the storm packed a punch, downing utility lines and trees, leading to power outages and road closures.

The freezing rain and gusty winds that followed that evening didn't help.

The city road crews in Holly Pointe had the streets into town open late Thursday afternoon. Trevor headed to the Barns to see if Lucy needed any help.

He found her sitting at her desk in her office, head in her hands. "Luce, what's wrong?"

She looked up, and he saw the lines of stress and fatigue edging her eyes. "The wedding was canceled."

"Why?" True bafflement filled Trevor's tone. "The roads are open."

"Here in town, but there are a lot in the rest of the state that are still closed." Lucy leaned back in her desk chair and expelled a heavy breath. "They've just begun clearing the airport runways in Burlington. Even if the bride and groom can get here, they're concerned about their family and friends making it."

"What are you going to do?"

She looked at him as if he'd spoken in a foreign language she didn't comprehend.

"I assume you can keep their deposit, but—"

"Yes, I'll keep the deposit." She apparently had spoken more sharply than she'd intended, because she held up a hand. "I'm sorry. Give me a minute."

Trevor wished he could put his arms around her and somehow make this all better. Unfortunately, he didn't possess those superpowers.

Lucy pinched the bridge of her nose for several seconds, then appeared to steady. "I'd just finished crunching the numbers when you walked in." She chuckled. "If I don't eat in January, I should still be able to make it."

He sensed that in this moment Lucy didn't need—or want—platitudes. Instead, Trevor went for humor. "I happen to know a guy who'd be happy to take you out for dinner every night in January."

That tugged a smile from her lips. "I might just hold you to it."

Leaning forward, he kissed her gently on the mouth. "It would be my pleasure."

Lucy's arms wound around his neck, and she kissed him back. She let out a sigh when their lips parted, her fingers sliding into his hair. "Until this moment, I hadn't realized how much I've missed being with you this week."

He'd missed her, too. It had never been like this with Anna Beth, Trevor realized. He could go days without seeing or talking with her and barely give her a second thought.

Lucy was always on his mind.

Trevor scattered kisses across her face and neck, wanting her with ever atom of his being. "Let's go upstairs to the apartment. I'll rub your back, and we can—"

The ringing of her phone startled both of them, and they sprang apart.

Removing her arms from around his neck, Lucy answered the phone and put it on speaker. "This is Lucy Cummings."

"Ms. Cummings, this is Harold Miesbach with Burton Coffee Roasters."

So much for relaxed. Trevor watched as tension once again furrowed Lucy's brow.

"Mr. Miesbach, how nice to hear from you." Lucy straightened and appeared to force even more cheer into her voice. "I'm happy to report that it appears the roads should be cleared for your weekend festivities. We—"

"Ms. Cummings, I'm afraid we've made the decision to cancel."

Though her voice remained calm, Lucy's hand trembled. "I'm afraid I don't understand. Why would you cancel?"

"The weather was the deciding factor."

"But...but..." Lucy took in a deep breath as if needing to get her thoughts and emotions under control. "Everything is being cleared now. The roads will be open."

"Yes, well, the board decided we can't take that chance." Miesbach continued without giving her a chance to respond. "We've had our attorney review the contract, and we understand that we will forfeit our deposit."

Lucy shut her eyes and appeared to fight for control. "Perhaps you'd like to wait until tomorrow, see how the roads look and make your decision then."

"We've already decided and are in the process of making alternative plans here in Burlington." The older man's businesslike tone softened. "We were looking forward to coming to Holly Pointe. We certainly will keep you in mind for future events."

Lucy sensed that to argue further would only alienate the man. "I appreciate you letting me know."

"You have yourself a wonderful holiday."

"You, too." Lucy clicked off the call, and the phone slid from her hand onto the tabletop. She turned to Trevor. "It's over. Without the full revenue from their event, I'll never have the money I need."

Trevor slipped his arms around her and held her close. "It will be okay."

Lucy jerked from Trevor's embrace and flung out her hands. "Weren't you listening? They canceled. First, the wedding canceled, now the Burton Coffee Roasters. It's done. Over. There is no way I can make up for this loss. Not in time."

"Go to the community. Ask for help."

"What? No." Lucy shook her head violently.

"Why not?"

"The community is mad at me for canceling the Mistletoe Ball in order to have a revenue-generating event to begin with."

"They'll want to help." Trevor's tone turned persuasive. "Just give them a chance. We can—"

"What do you know about this community?" Lucy fought for control, but quickly lost the battle. "You haven't been here for fifteen years. You left, Trevor, and you didn't come back until last month." She flung the words at him as the anger and hurt of his leaving all those years ago rose like hot bile to scorch her throat. "You left not only your grandmother, but you left me. You just left."

She strode to the window and put her hands on the sill, her breath heaving in and out as if she'd just run a long race.

Trevor stood behind her for several long seconds, but when he placed a hand on her shoulder, she whirled, and it dropped to his side.

"I know the people in this town better than you do. You don't know what you're talking about."

All her life, Lucy had lost the things she loved—her childhood best friend, Kevin and now her business. Each time, she found a way to move forward on her own. Today would be no different.

"I just need to think right now, Trevor. This is my problem, and I'll solve it myself, like I always have. And I can't do that with you here. You need to leave. You already know how." The second the words left her mouth, Lucy realized she wasn't being fair. But she didn't have the remaining composure right now to take back the hurtful words.

He stared at her for a long moment. Then his gaze hardened,

and a muscle jumped in his jaw. When he finally spoke, his voice was gravelly.

"I don't force myself where I'm not wanted, so I'll do as you ask and leave."

A second later, the door slammed shut behind him.

CHAPTER TWENTY-ONE

An hour later, Lucy found herself sitting across from Melinda at the diner. The cheerful Christmas tunes playing overhead scraped against her nerves like a rusty knife on raw flesh.

"I'm sorry, Lucy." Leaning forward, Mel blanketed her hand for a quick squeeze. "Two cancellations in twenty-four hours sucks."

Lucy took a sip of her Green River, a lemon-lime drink that was colored green. It had been a favorite since childhood. She'd loved when Hedy would bring her and Trevor to the diner and buy them each one.

She took a long sip and decided that what the drink needed, what she needed, was a healthy dose of vodka. "Trevor and I are done."

"Wh-what?" Melinda set down her drink. "Why?"

"Well..." Lucy could have cheered when her voice came out casual and offhand, just as she'd intended. "I've got too much going on. I don't need the stress."

Mel made a give-me-more gesture with one hand. "That doesn't cut it."

"He doesn't understand me."

"Phsst."

The dismissive sound had Lucy's frown deepening. "What do you mean by that?"

"He loves you, Lucy. Everyone can see it."

"Maybe I don't love him."

Mel rolled her eyes. "You do, and we both know it."

"I don't want to talk about Trevor."

"You're the one who brought him up," Mel pointed out.

"My mistake." Thinking of Trevor made her want to weep, so Lucy determinedly pushed thoughts of him aside.

"If you don't want to talk about him, let's talk about how you're going to save the Barns. You'll have a plan. You always have a plan."

"Trevor thinks I need to rally the town," Lucy told her friend. "I wasn't sure about it at the time. Actually, I snapped at him for mentioning it, which I shouldn't have done. But the more I think about it, the more I realize the idea has merit."

"I think it's an excellent idea." Melinda leaned forward, her hazel eyes snapping. "What's our first step?"

Trevor swung by the Candy Cane Christmas House to pick up his grandmother after she texted him that activities had been canceled for the day.

On the drive home, he listened to Hedy tell him about all the cookies that had been collected for a cookie exchange tomorrow.

"Hopefully the roads will stay cleared. If not, Mary might need to freeze those cookies." Hedy laughed. "We'll be eating Christmas cookies until Easter."

His grandmother had been all smiles when he'd picked her up. Her happy nature was only one of the things Trevor admired about her. For a woman who'd lost a husband at a relatively young age, then ended up with a daughter who'd caused her no end of grief, she'd still managed to keep that sunny nature.

Once they were at her house and taking off their coats, Trevor turned to her. "Can I make you some tea?"

"Only if you'll join me."

Trevor made them each a cup, then sat on the sofa while she took the straight-backed chair with the cushioned bottom and arms that had always been her favorite.

"I realized as you were making the tea that I've been chattering nonstop since you picked me up." Hedy sipped the peppermint tea she preferred, then sighed. "This is so good. Thank you."

"I didn't much care for it when I first got here," Trevor admitted. "It's growing on me."

"I'm surprised you aren't with Lucy." Hedy's brows pulled together. "Then again, I'm sure she's busy putting the final touches on the big corporate event. Knowing her, she's determined to make every detail perfect."

"You haven't heard?" Trevor glanced at Hedy over the rim of his mug.

Hedy lowered her cup, something in his tone obviously putting her on alert. "Heard what?"

"The Burton Coffee Roasters canceled."

"They did what?" Hedy set her cup on the saucer she held in her other hand with such force that tea sloshed over the rim. "Why would they cancel? The roads are opening up, and they've revised the forecast for less snowfall."

"That's what Lucy told them when they called." Trevor felt sick inside as he remembered the look on Lucy's face. "They didn't care. They'd decided to cancel, and they did."

"That poor girl." Worry blanketed Hedy's face. "What's she going to do without that money?"

"Not my problem." Trevor shrugged. He'd like to believe that Lucy's rejection hadn't hurt, but he would be kidding himself.

Being shut out of her life at a time when she needed him most hurt. A lot.

"What kind of response is that?"

Hedy's sharp tone had Trevor looking up from his tea. He hadn't heard that tone since he'd been eleven and had let the neighbor's dog out of the backyard, and it had run off.

Thankfully, that story had had a happy ending. Unlike him and Lucy.

"An honest one." Trevor set down his mug. "I suggested she enlist the community to help. I offered to help her do that. She rejected the idea without even considering it fully. Then she went off on me for leaving all those years ago, as if that was my fault." He felt a muscle in his jaw jump.

"I'm sure the phone call upset her," Hedy said. "She's been trying so hard—"

"I've been trying, too. Trying hard to build a relationship with her. She obviously doesn't want that." Even as he forced a bored tone, Trevor's heart twisted. "Trevor Sherwood doesn't stay where he's not wanted."

Hedy studied him for a long moment, then expelled a sigh. "I didn't think you were like your mother. Now, I'm wondering if I was mistaken."

Trevor stiffened. "That's a lousy thing to say. I'm not anything like my mom."

"I don't think you mean to be. I—"

"I'm not." He lifted his chin, daring her to say more.

"I believe you don't want to be like her."

Trevor opened his mouth to once again say he wasn't, then snapped it shut, reminding himself it had been said once, so there was no need to belabor the point.

Besides, did his grandmother really think he was like Angie?

"We both know Mom isn't reliable." Trevor spoke coolly in an attempt to hide his hurt. "I would hope that isn't how you view me."

Picking up her cup, Hedy took a long sip as if carefully considering her next words. "I believe you've spent your life trying to prove that you aren't like her."

"I'm *not* like her."

Hedy continued as if he hadn't spoken. "You entered into a serious relationship with a woman back in Tennessee. I'm only speculating, but I'd guess becoming so serious with a woman you ultimately didn't love was an attempt to prove to yourself that you didn't jump from partner to partner."

Trevor shifted uncomfortably on the sofa cushions.

"Now that you're back in Holly Pointe, you've tried to do your best for me and Lucy."

"Lucy made it very clear that she doesn't need or want me."

"The thing is, Trevor, what you're showing me now is that you *are* like your mother."

He clenched his jaw. "I don't understand how you can say that."

"My Angie was a partier. While that was an issue, the real problem with her, as I see it, was that when things got hard, she left. Lucy's mom did the same." Hedy's eyes turned as soft as her voice. "Right now, things are hard with Lucy. And now you tell me you're leaving her—"

"Don't you understand?" His voice rose despite his best efforts to control it. "She doesn't want me."

Hedy waved a dismissive hand. "We both know that isn't true. Lucy loves you. Like I said, things are hard for that sweet girl right now. You need to stay and do the hard. You need to be there for her."

Trevor sipped his tea, not sure what he wanted to say, not sure what there was to say.

"This isn't about reliability, it's about toughness." Hedy met his gaze. "Your mother didn't tough it out. If you want to prove that you're not like her, don't walk away from a good woman just because things have gotten difficult."

Hedy's eyes blazed as she leaned forward, her gaze never leaving his face. "See this through. Stay and fight for what you love and want."

～

For over an hour, Lucy sat with Mel and plotted strategy. They came up with a whole list of ways to raise money. The only problem was they all depended on community volunteers.

When Lucy thought of everything that needed to be done before Christmas, she felt overwhelmed. So much to do and so little time.

Mel had promised to make up some flyers, and Stella would do a news blast on the town's social media sites. Lucy was to drum up volunteers and secure prizes.

She vowed to ask every single businessperson she ran across for their help. The first person she ran across was Calvin Burkey.

Putting a smile on her face, Lucy lifted a hand as the town's large-animal vet drew close. "Dr. Burkey, do you have a moment?"

Lucy quickly explained what she was planning. "Would you be interested in volunteering? We'll need lots of volunteers to make this work."

"I'm sorry, Lucy, but I still haven't gotten over you canceling the Mistletoe Ball. I expressed my concerns, but you weren't about to change your mind." Cal shook his head. "You know how I felt about Kevin."

Cal and Kevin had bonded over their love of horses.

"Kevin was such a good man," Cal continued. "He loved Christmas and the Mistletoe Ball. Canceling the party defiled his memory."

As Lucy had already explained why she'd had to cancel the Mistletoe Ball, she saw no reason to go down that road again. Now that the Big Barn was available, there was a chance they might be able to pull together some kind of party for Saturday night.

Until Lucy had the details worked out and knew for sure it would work, she wouldn't get his hopes up. "Thank you anyway. Merry Christmas."

"Merry Christmas to you, too."

Lucy had barely gone a few feet when she ran into Larry Kotopka. She considered Larry to be a reasonable man. A life-long resident, a father and a grandfather, he'd been active in the Holly Pointe community for decades. His vehemence surrounding the ball and his argument that a person never knew if they'd be around next year had made her wonder if either he or his wife, LouAnn, had some medical condition that hadn't been made public. She certainly hoped that wasn't the case.

After once again going through what was planned and asking if he'd like to contribute, Larry shook his head. "Normally, I'd help you out, Lucy, but this whole Mistletoe Ball cancellation left me and the wife with a sour taste."

Well, that was clear enough.

Two strikes, Lucy thought, as she continued down the street. At the rate she was going, she might strike out before she reached her car.

When she saw Indigo headed her way, Lucy nearly turned and headed the other way. *Not a quitter*, she told herself.

She plastered a bright smile on her face. "Indigo, it's good to see you." Lucy gestured to the bags the woman held. "Looks like you're doing some Christmas shopping."

Indigo lifted one bag with the Pawsibilities store logo on the front. "Almost done."

"I have something I'd like to ask you."

The older woman inclined her head. "I'm listening."

"The company that had rented the Barns for this weekend pulled out. If I can't make up the lost revenue, I won't be able to purchase the Barns next month, and someone who doesn't know or love Holly Pointe might buy Grace Hollow."

The older woman, her gray-streaked hair pulled back in a long tail, wrinkles lining her weathered face, shook her head, a pitying look in her eyes. "That's what happens when you sell your soul to the corporate devils."

"Ah, yes, well, here's the deal. Tomorrow, we're going to be creating what we're calling the Reindeer Games for kids six through sixteen. I was hoping I could count on you to volunteer."

"I find it odd that you ask me to help you when you weren't interested in helping those of us who wanted to keep the Mistletoe Ball going." Indigo huffed out a breath. "Frankly, I don't know why I would help you."

Lucy braced herself, knowing the woman was only getting geared up. In past encounters, no matter what explanations she'd offered, Indigo hadn't been inclined to listen.

"You should help her, because that's what people in this town do." Trevor stepped forward. "Capital of Christmas Kindness and all that. What happened to that?"

To Lucy's surprise, redness that had nothing to do with the cold rose up Indigo's neck. "But canceling the ball—"

"A necessity to keep the Barns under local control," Trevor responded without missing a beat. "Lucy is doing her best to make sure that happens. She cares about this community and about you."

Indigo shifted her gaze to Lucy. "The events are being held tomorrow?"

"Yes. In the morning." Lucy proceeded with caution. "Would you be available to help?"

"I'll be there. You have my contact information on the vendor list. Text me where and when, and I'll be there." Indigo appeared to be avoiding looking in Trevor's direction. "I'll see you both then."

Lucy waited until Indigo was out of earshot before pulling

Trevor into the Busy Bean. She saw with a quick glance the long line at the counter. She didn't give it a second thought. She wasn't here for a latte. She was here for answers.

"What are you doing?"

"Well, at this moment, I'm standing in a coffee shop."

Lucy scowled. "No, why are you helping? I can do this on my own. Did you think I couldn't handle Indigo?"

"I didn't think that at all." Those deep-brown eyes searched hers. "You seem to have all these ideas about needing to be independent, of how things are supposed to be, about how you're supposed to be."

"I don't know what you're talking about," Lucy shot back, but deep down, her insides quivered in understanding.

"Don't worry about what things are supposed to be like, Luce. You were supposed to be with Kevin, but you're not. I was supposed to marry Anna Beth, but I didn't. We were supposed to have mothers we could depend on, and look how that went. You've got this image of yourself as someone who has to go it alone, but give yourself permission to change." His gaze softened, and something in his earnest expression touched her heart. "You're an independent woman. You have always been an independent problem solver. You won't stop being those things by letting me be part of your team."

CHAPTER TWENTY-TWO

"If you raised the age to thirty, we could compete." Trevor kept his gaze on the top of the hill and his ear peeled for the starting whistle.

"You and I will find a time to compete," Lucy assured him, her focus remaining on the pink sled poised for takeoff.

The last-minute, pulled-together Reindeer Games were an unqualified hit. The events had been arranged in less than twenty-four hours, but thanks to a media blitz, including Dustin and Krista doing a television interview on AM Burlington, parents had brought their kids to Holly Pointe in droves.

Of course, the fact that anyone placing second or third in their age division got a hundred dollars and anyone placing first could choose between two hundred dollars and a private hockey lesson with former NHL superstar Dustin Bellamy had definitely sparked interest. No one batted an eye at the twenty-dollar entry fee.

With the prize money being covered by various prominent Holly Pointe businesses in exchange for promotion, there was no cost outlay.

The shrill sound of the whistle split the air, and Lucy hit her stopwatch. The cheers and voices screaming encouragement from the sidelines were music to her ears. Not only because the sounds brought back pleasant memories from the games Hedy had dreamed up, but because these games added to the holiday excitement in Holly Pointe.

More tourists had shown up, which meant money going into the coffers of all the businesses.

Lucy hit her stopwatch as the girl on the pink sled crossed the finish line and called out, "Great job!"

"Did I win?" The child, who couldn't have been more than six, looked up at Lucy with eyes as blue as the sky overhead.

"There are more heats to run," she told the girl. "But you won a cookie just by competing."

She handed the child a Christmas cookie decorated with red icing and a Santa on the front. Wrapped in cellophane, it was tied with a pretty ribbon. This addition to the Reindeer Games had been Camryn's brainchild.

The young teen and her friends had gotten together with Mary at the Candy Cane Christmas House to make the cookies happen.

The child gazed, wide-eyed, at the cookie. Her parents, who'd approached to gather up her and the sled, smiled and prompted, "What do you say, Ellie?"

"Thank you." Ellie's gaze remained on the cookie.

"We're from Montpelier. We've thought about coming to Holly Pointe for a number of years, but just never made it," the mother confided. "When we heard about the Reindeer Games, Joe and I knew the kids would love it."

"Our son is competing in the nine-to-twelve age bracket," the father said. "He's hoping to win the hockey lesson."

"Well, win or lose, he'll have fun." Lucy lifted a hand in farewell as the parents strolled off with their child.

Lucy turned to Trevor. Behind them, the sounds of the high school's Triple Trio singing Christmas carols added a festive element to the scene.

"I wonder if we'll get as good of a response to the Rockin' Reindeer Bash at the Barn tonight." Lucy hoped that making the event casual and having an aspiring DJ spin the tunes would work.

"Asking Larry Kotopka's grandson to be the DJ was inspired." Trevor chuckled. "The man went from being a Grinch to be totally in."

"The best part is Larry will make sure the young man plays tunes that will appeal to everyone present."

"I think the best part is being able to use the food and decorations that Burton Coffee Roasters couldn't cancel at the last minute." Trevor grinned.

"Which makes whatever we get from the ticket sales pure profit."

"Will it be enough?" Trevor's expression turned serious.

"I don't know. I hope so." The sounds of "Rockin' Around the Christmas Tree" ended, and Lucy stepped back into position.

As she glanced around, she realized that regardless of what happened, she was blessed. Her community had come together in a big way to help.

If the money raised wasn't enough to help her reach her goal, she would have to be thankful for the effort.

Lucy studied the barn. The red-and-white checkerboard dance floor with trees decorated in red and silver might not have been the way she'd have chosen to decorate, but she had to admit the Burton Coffee Roasters decorations were perfect for the Rockin' Reindeer Bash.

As she and her volunteer crew were applying the finishing touches, she stopped Zach and his friends from taking down a huge banner that proclaimed, "Burton Coffee Roasters: Good for Vermont and the World."

"Leave it up." At his quizzical look, she shrugged. "They were kind enough to let us use their decorations and food. It's a way for us to thank them."

"They left you in the lurch," Zach pointed out.

"They gave me an opportunity to think outside the box." Lucy glanced over to where Trevor was working with Logan Kotopka on getting his equipment set up. She thought of the Reindeer Games this morning and the number of business owners who'd thanked her for the increased traffic to their stores. "Seeing all of us coming together solidifies what everyone who lives here has always known—we are stronger together."

Zach clapped her on the back. "You've changed, Lucy girl."

Ignoring the puzzling remark, Lucy strode across the room to where Stella stood, taking photos of the ballroom for the town's social media sites. Stella turned to Lucy with a questioning glance. "You left the Burton sign up?"

Lucy wondered how many times she'd have to explain that decision this evening. "They graciously allowed us to use their food and decorations."

"After canceling at the last minute."

"Like I told Zach, because of this hiccup, I realized that Holly Pointe is not only the Capital of Christmas Kindness, we're the Capital of Christmas Togetherness."

Stella shot her a skeptical look. "Nice thought, but that hiccup, as you call it, may have torpedoed your ability to buy the Barns."

"Maybe." Lucy kept her tone matter-of-fact. "I've done what I can. *We've* done all we can. Now, we just wait."

"And while we wait?" Stella arched a brow.

"We party like there's no tomorrow."

◠

All it took, Trevor thought, for all to be right in his world was having Lucy in his arms. They'd been so busy they hadn't really had an opportunity to talk, so he wasn't sure if everything was back to normal between them or not. Right now, it felt that way.

As they danced to one of the songs in the slow set that Logan had included in his playlist, Trevor let his gaze skim the dance floor. Though promoted as a casual, fun holiday event, some attendees had still chosen to dress up in their Christmas finery. Others wore jeans and sweaters, a good number of them even wearing "ugly sweaters."

The one thing all the attendees had in common—happy smiles. Logan, despite a few missteps, was doing an excellent job reading the audience and appeared to be having a blast as DJ.

Lowering the minimum age to attend to twelve had brought in a good number of middle schoolers, most of whom had arrived with their parents, then flocked to hang out with their friends.

"This party is amazing," Trevor whispered against her hair. "All because of you."

She was shaking her head even before she tipped it back to look up at him.

"This was a true team effort." Her eyes met his. "You helped me see that it's okay to reach out for help. For that, I'll be forever grateful."

"I don't want your gratitude, Luce." His voice deepened with emotion. "I want—"

"Lucy." Stella's voice had them both turning in the pretty brunette's direction. "You mentioned wanting to address the crowd. As the night is winding down, this may be a good time."

Lucy turned to Trevor and kissed him on the mouth. "Hold that thought. I'll be right back."

"She's an amazing woman," Stella murmured.

Trevor let his gaze follow Lucy through the crowd. She was a beautiful woman, but tonight she looked especially adorable in her blue snowflake leggings topped with a fluffy blue sweater. Blonde curls spilled over her shoulders.

Mine, he thought, but he knew, even as the emotion threatened to choke him, that maybe she wasn't his. Maybe she never would be.

What he did know was that he loved her, that he wanted to be with her forever. Not to prove that he wasn't like his mother, or to prove that he could stick, but because he couldn't imagine his life without Lucy in it.

On her way to the stage, Lucy spotted Alice Roth, a reporter from Montpelier, dancing with Craig Stanton, a reporter with the *Burlington Free Press*.

When Lucy paused beside them, they stopped dancing. She offered a cheery smile. "I won't keep you, but I wanted to personally thank you both for helping to publicize the Reindeer Games and tonight's event."

"My pleasure." Craig, a tall man in his sixties, gave a nod.

Alice, a sharp-featured woman with a liberal amount of gray in her dark hair, studied Lucy. "I understand that if you don't raise enough money from these two events the Barns at Grace Hollow could be sold to an out-of-state buyer. Is that true?"

"It is, but I'm not going to worry about that tonight." Lucy somehow managed a smile. "Thanks again for all you've done."

She reached the stage as the current melody was drawing to an end. Catching Logan's eye, she motioned for him to hold the next song.

"Hello, everyone, and thank you for coming to our first ever

Rockin' Reindeer Bash." She scanned the crowd. "Are you having fun?"

A large roar echoed through the room, and Lucy grinned.

"That's what I like to hear. I'll let you get back to the fun, but I'd like us to give a big round of applause to those who made this event happen on such short notice. There are too many of you to name individually, but you know who you are, and just know that this wouldn't have happened without you."

Applause, cheers and a few shrill whistles filled the air. When the din quieted, Lucy gestured with her hand to the Burton Coffee Roasters sign. "I'd also like to thank the Burton Coffee Roasters. They are a Vermont company with deep roots in our state. They had to cancel their Christmas event, but allowed us to use their fabulous decorations and food to make our event even more special. Thank you, Burton Coffee Roasters."

Lucy left the stage to more applause and cheers.

It took her a while to reach Trevor. Every few feet, she was stopped by someone wanting to thank her for either the Reindeer Games or tonight's event, often both.

Despite her words on the stage, everyone seemed to think she'd pulled this together single-handedly, when nothing could have been further from the truth. But Lucy smiled graciously, keeping Trevor in sight.

By the time she reached him, Logan had announced the final song, "Believe" from the movie *The Polar Express*.

Lucy smiled at Trevor and held out her arms. "May I have this dance?"

When he wrapped his arms around her and they began to sway, Lucy rested her head against his chest and relaxed fully.

Listening to the words, Lucy realized she knew what her heart was saying. She could lose the Barns, but she couldn't lose this man.

She just had to believe that he wanted her as much as she wanted him.

∽

Trevor glanced around the now-empty ballroom. Once the party had ended, Lucy had insisted all the helpers head directly home instead of staying to help clean up.

Lucy hadn't said she wanted him to leave. Then again, she hadn't asked him to stay.

He saw the fatigue in the lines around her eyes and the slump of her shoulders when she strode over to him. "The night couldn't have gone better."

"We pulled it off." Pride filled Trevor's voice.

We. Thinking of the two of them together came so naturally.

Hope surged when she smiled.

Then she pulled out a chair and sat.

He did the same. "Do you have any idea how much money was raised between this and the Reindeer Games?"

"You mean, is it enough?"

He nodded.

"I don't know." She expelled a heavy breath and raked a hand through her hair. "Right now, I'm too tired to care."

Perhaps, but he knew how much these Barns mattered to her.

"You should get home. Hedy—"

"Is spending the night with Mary at the Christmas House," Trevor finished for her. "With Faith and Graham stuck in New York because of the weather, Mary would have been spending the weekend alone."

Trevor hesitated, then took the polar plunge. "I hoped I'd be spending the night with you."

She studied him with those incredible blue eyes. "We've never talked about our fight."

"You mean the one where you accused me of leaving this community and never looking back? The one where you said I wasn't the boss of you? That one?"

"Yeah, that one."

"All true," he admitted. "I'm not the boss of you, and I did leave."

"I was wrong to say that because you didn't have a choice. You were wrong though, about something you said."

He wasn't sure where she was going with this. "What was that?"

"You said I didn't want you."

Everything in Trevor froze.

"I not only want you, I love you." Lucy gave an embarrassed laugh. "I've spent so many years trying to prove I don't need anyone, but the truth is, I need you, Trevor. You make me happy, and I can't imagine my life without you in it."

"I have a gift for you."

She blinked. "What?"

"A Christmas gift. It's out in my car." He pushed back the chair and rose. "I'll get it."

"You don't have to—" she began, but he was already out the door.

Lucy fought the tears that sprang to her eyes. She'd bared her soul, her heart, to Trevor, and not only hadn't he shared his feelings with her, he'd changed the subject to Christmas gifts.

She buried her face in her hands.

When she heard his footsteps, she looked up to see him carrying a huge box wrapped in red paper and topped with a candy-striped bow.

"I don't have a gift for you," she said. "I planned to get something for you, but—"

"No worries." He cleared the table in front of her with one hand, then set the box down. "Merry Christmas, Lucy."

Under his expectant gaze, Lucy removed the ribbon, then

carefully unwrapped the package. With fingers that trembled, she lifted off the lid…and gaped.

A massive wreath carved out of wood sat in a bed of tissue. At the base of the wreath where a ribbon would be was her face. All around the perimeter of the wreath were the faces of people important in her life: Hedy and Kevin, Mel and Kate. Even Paula.

Her gaze lingered on the image of her mother.

"Family is family, even when they're imperfect." Trevor's gaze never left hers. "I wasn't sure who all you'd want, so there's plenty of room to add. I see the wreath as a circle, a symbol of our connectiveness."

"It's beautiful." She touched the images reverently with the tips of her fingers. "Incredible."

Trevor's lips curved upward. "You like it?"

"I love it." She met his gaze. "But why did you leave off your face?"

"I didn't know if you'd want it there."

"I think the better question is, do you want it there?" Lucy cleared her throat. "Do you want to be part of my circle?"

The answering smile that spread over his face eased the tightness gripping her chest.

"I love you, Lucy. I want more than anything to be a permanent part of your life. I want to grow old with you, have children with you, marry you." Reaching into his pocket, he pulled out a jeweler's case and flipped it open with his thumb. "Will you marry me, Luce? Will you be my friend, my lover, my wife?"

She gazed down at the ring, then looked up at him. "You got me another gift."

A startled look crossed his face. Then, something he must have seen on her face, or maybe it was the love that she knew had to be shining in her eyes, had him grinning and sweetening the pot. "I'll give you the win when we compete in the next Reindeer Games if you say yes."

Lucy flung her arms around his neck and kissed him with all the love in her heart.

"Yes," she whispered against his lips when they came up for air. "I'll marry you. But forget about spotting me in the Reindeer Games. If I win, it will be because I earned it."

Trevor laughed, the sound one of pure joy. "Have it your way. I'd say, in this case, we both win."

EPILOGUE

Lucy had crunched the numbers every way she could think of, and despite the considerable money raised from the Reindeer Games and the Christmas Eve party, she was still short of the amount she needed to secure the loan.

When learning of her plight, Geoff and Emily, as well as Dustin and Krista, offered her the funds she needed. So far, Lucy had resisted accepting their money.

She would take the money—then repay it—before she'd let the Barns go to someone else, but she hoped to find a way to do it on her own before going that route.

A knock on the door to her office had her looking up to find Trevor standing in the doorway. "You're back."

"It doesn't take long to close out an apartment when there's not much there." He dropped down into her visitor's chair. "Closing up my shop in Knoxville took a little more time. All I need to do is find shop space for my tools."

He'd flown down to Knoxville five days ago. The last two had been spent driving back to Vermont with his tools in a U-Haul. Though they'd spoken frequently, it hadn't been the same as seeing his smiling face each morning.

With Hedy's blessing, Trevor had moved in with Lucy. The plan was for a small, intimate wedding ceremony in the Baby Barn on January twenty-eighth.

Neither of them wanted to wait.

"I missed you, Trev."

He chuckled. "You sound surprised."

She shook her head. "I knew I'd miss you. I just wasn't prepared for how much."

"Same for me." He dropped a pile of envelopes onto the desk. "I grabbed the mail on my way inside."

Lucy noticed the top envelope held a Burton Coffee Roasters return address. Lifting it, she showed it to Trevor. "I wonder why they're contacting me."

"No time like the present to find out."

As Lucy opened the envelope, a check fell to the table. It was made out to her, and the amount would more than cover what she needed to qualify for the loan.

She studied the check, then lifted the envelope and took out a folded sheet of paper. Lucy read the letter, then reread it. She set the single sheet on the desk, momentarily too stunned to speak.

Worry furrowed Trevor's brow as he skirted the desk to stand at her side. "What does it say?"

"Mr. Miesbach says to consider the check a thank-you for the advertising I gave the company when I made my speech. Apparently, a photo of the banner I'd left up was shared online, and the company was mentioned in the articles the reporters did on the event."

"You did them a solid, so they're doing one for you."

Lucy picked up the check, and her fingers began to tremble. She gazed at Trevor. "You know what this means?"

"That you can buy the Barns."

"I can buy the Barns," Lucy repeated.

"You're getting everything you ever wanted." He pulled her to him and brushed a kiss across her lips. "I'm so happy for you."

"I already have everything I want." Cupping his cheek, Lucy gazed into the eyes of the man she loved. "Having you in my life is everything. Owning the Barns, well, that will be the cherry atop a very delicious sundae."

Trevor laughed. "So now I'm a sundae?"

"A very delicious sundae," she reminded him, then glanced out the window. "Look. It's snowing again."

Trevor tugged her to her feet and wrapped his arms around her. "It's like I've always said. There's snow place like Holly Pointe."

Lucy was still laughing when his mouth closed over hers.

I'm so happy you got to see Lucy and Trevor find love and their own happy ending after so many years apart.

If you love heartwarming holiday romance, you're going to want to take a trip back to the first book in the Holly Pointe series, *Home for the Holly Days*, which takes place nearly ten years before Holly Pointe & Mistletoe, the first book in the series.

This award-winning, uplifting romance is Dustin and Krista's love story and is sure to keep you reading WAY too late at night.

Buy *Home for the Holly Days* to unwrap this festive love story today or keep reading for a sneak peek.

SNEAK PEEK OF HOME FOR THE HOLLY DAYS

Chapter 1

Krista Ankrom gazed out the restaurant's ninth-floor window at the festive scene below. The Norway spruce decorated for Christmas stood tall and majestic in Rockefeller Center. The splendor of its 50,000 LED lights was surpassed only by the Swarovski star at the top. Krista remembered a news anchor mentioning yesterday at the tree lighting that the star was covered with three million crystals.

The gorgeous scene should have buoyed her flagging spirits, as should this impromptu lunch with her friend.

Across the table, Desz Presley answered work emails and sipped her drink. It was a given that when she and Desz visited L'Avenue for lunch, her friend would multitask while enjoying sea bass and an Aperol Spritz.

Krista returned her attention to the tree covered in multicolored lights, the throngs of tourists skating in front of it, and the Salvation Army Santa on the corner. An engaging scene straight out of a Hallmark movie. Most years, she lovingly drank it in.

"Krista? Are you listening?"

"Hmmm? What? Sorry, Desz. I spaced out watching the skaters." Krista waved an airy hand, not wanting to burden her friend with her thoughts.

"What, you mean you weren't riveted by me complaining about my parents again?"

Though Desz had fully embraced life in NYC since moving here three years ago, at Christmas she loved going home to Tennessee and her family's lavish Christmas celebrations. This year, Desz's parents had opted for a cruise, leaving Desz to spend Christmas in the city.

"I know how you feel." Krista pulled her gaze from the window to give her friend her full attention. "I hoped my family would come spend Christmas with me this year. But Tom and his wife just had their first child, and traveling with a baby can be difficult."

Desz took another sip of her drink. "Remind me why you aren't going there?"

"I considered it until I learned Claire's parents are also spending the holidays with them. It'll be a full house." Krista lifted her glass of spring water. "It figures the one year I'm free, enjoying a family Christmas isn't an option."

"You've always worked over the holidays." Desz sipped her drink, a thoughtful look creasing her brow. "Or you have every year since we first met."

"I planned to get the Japan job and be in Tokyo this month. Not meant to be." Krista had known the repeatedly delayed contract offer had been a bad sign. It didn't matter what her agent, Merline, said about age being no cause for concern, at twenty-eight, Krista understood the realities of her situation.

She'd been right to be concerned. The model chosen to be the new face of Shibusa Cosmetics was a decade younger than she was.

"You'll get another account. A bigger, better one." Desz's voice rang with confidence. "Shibusa will regret not choosing you."

Krista lifted her water in a toast. "I'll drink to that."

Her mocking tone had Desz chuckling before she changed the subject. "At least your parents are staying home to spend Christmas with their first grandchild. My parents are choosing a seafood buffet on the lido deck over me. In what world is that tradition?"

Krista laughed. "No more than working over the holidays can be considered a tradition."

"I'd say you're due for a change." Desz's dark eyes sparkled. "You're an independent woman with enough money to do whatever you want. You should go somewhere. Hey, what am I saying? *We* should go somewhere. Where do you want to go? Totally your call."

An image of the quaint community she'd loved near the Canadian border flashed in Krista's mind. "It's not a place you'd be interested in."

Desz leaned forward. "You let me decide."

"Holly Pointe." Simply saying the name brought a smile to Krista's lips. "Before I got my first big modeling contract and moved to New York, my family spent every Christmas in Vermont."

"Holly Pointe, Vermont." Desz rolled the name around on her tongue, then smiled. "I've never been that far north."

"It's lovely there." Krista sighed. "A picture postcard of how life can be."

Desz cocked her head. "Huh?"

"People in Holly Pointe care about one another. Everyone takes time to enjoy the holidays." Krista smiled, remembering all the events. "There's always a big tree lighting, followed by caroling in the town square. Santa is, well, everywhere. All the buildings are decorated and—"

Krista stopped herself, recalling the elaborate traditions Desz had told her about in Nashville. "It's very humble compared to the Christmas celebrations you're used to."

"It sounds fabulous." Desz clasped her hands together. "I've never experienced a small-town Christmas."

It almost sounded as if Desz was open to going to Holly Pointe. Krista's smile grew. If she couldn't be with her family at Christmas, maybe being in a place that reminded her of them would be the next best thing.

"Does going there for several weeks sound like something you'd want to do?" Krista knew Desz could work from anywhere, and a few weeks someplace free of billboards and ad agencies might help her stop stressing about work.

"I can be packed and ready to leave tomorrow morning."

For the first time since learning she hadn't gotten the Shibusa account, Krista experienced a surge of holiday happiness. She lifted her glass. "To the best Christmas ever."

Desz clinked her glass against Krista's. "To new adventures."

Dustin Bellamy strode down Fifth Avenue, a man on a mission. Out of the corner of his eye, he saw a guy burst out of a store and barrel his way toward the curb where a cab had just pulled up.

The man brushed past him, would have clipped him, if Dustin's reflexes hadn't been good. Built like a bull, the guy reminded Dustin of Stan, a teammate. Stan with his hard wrist shot and a willingness to drop the gloves.

God, he missed his friends. Even the hot-tempered ones.

Lost in thought for several seconds, Dustin stood there while the crowd parted around him. Then he began walking, not wanting to keep the doctor waiting. Though Dustin had to sprint the last two blocks, he stepped off the elevator on the fifth floor with three minutes to spare.

The receptionist, an attractive woman with blonde hair, stood when Dustin entered.

"I'm Dustin Bellamy," he told her. "I have an appointment with Dr. Wallace."

"I know who you are," she said with a smile. "Let me show you the way."

Instead of an exam room, she ushered him into the doctor's luxurious private office.

She inclined her head. "May I get you something to drink while you wait?"

Dustin shook his head. "I'm fine. Thanks."

"The doctor should only be a few minutes." With the promise hanging in the air, she pulled the door closed behind her.

Restless, Dustin wandered the spacious area with its huge flat-screen TV and a standing desk in walnut. A wall of shelves near a sitting area held not only books, but medical awards and several modern sculptures of athletes.

Eric Wallace, orthopedic surgeon and sports medicine guru, had come highly recommended. Though only in his late forties, he was the team physician for several professional sports teams as well as numerous top athletes.

Dustin moved to the window and glanced down on the busy street below. He turned when he heard the door open, his heart kicking into high gear.

Tall and lean, the doctor moved with the grace of an athlete, holding out a hand as he crossed the last few feet to Dustin.

"Eric Wallace. It's a pleasure to finally meet you, Mr. Bellamy." His hand closed around Dustin's in a firm shake. "I'm a huge fan. Please, have a seat."

The doctor gestured to an area with several chairs and a small sofa. Dustin chose one, and the doctor sat in another opposite his.

After a few minutes of polite conversation, Dr. Wallace got down to business. "I reviewed your records and the most recent MRI. You're aware that normally the ACL tears when the muscles around the knee are weak. Because of all the skating you do, that isn't the case with you, not in regard to your previous injury or with this most recent one. Your tests show the muscles around your knee are well-developed and strong. But hockey puts a lot of stress on the ligament due to the twisting, pivoting and cutting."

"The original tear was from a collision with another player," Dustin offered, though the information was in the records.

Wallace nodded. "After the first injury, it appears you had excellent surgical results from the tendon graft."

"I worked hard at rehab." Dustin kept his attention on the doctor's face, searching for the slightest hint of encouragement. "After seven months of intense work, I was back to a hundred percent when I returned to the ice."

The doctor nodded, his expression softening. "I watched the game where you were checked. You kept playing despite reinjuring the ligament."

"It was the first game of the finals." Dustin lifted his chin to meet the doctor's questioning gaze head on. "The trainers braced the knee."

"I'm sure you were aware that playing with a damaged ACL opened you up to further injury." The doctor spoke in a matter-of-fact tone.

"My team needed me. We were in the playoffs." Dustin's breathing wanted to spike, but he kept it slow and easy. "I have no regrets. Winning the Cup was worth it. Since June, I've worked on staying fit and healthy. I can skate, but it's clear that without surgery I won't be able to get back to a competitive level."

Dr. Wallace sat back in his chair, regret blanketing his face. "I'm sorry, Dustin. I can't recommend another surgery."

"I don't think you understand. I'm willing—eager—to do whatever it takes." Dustin leaned forward. "What about platelet-rich plasma treatments to speed healing? I know you've used it on hockey players."

"PRP treatments can speed healing and stimulate tissue regeneration in the treated area after surgery. However, as I stated, I can't recommend a second ACL surgical intervention for you." Compassion filled the doctor's blue eyes. "Not based on the extent of your injury."

Dustin had to stop himself from jumping up and railing at the doctor. Didn't the man understand? Hockey was more than a game to him. It was his life.

Over the years, Dustin had become an expert at pushing past the pain. Most of the time, it was physical. Hockey—at any level, but especially at the highest level—was hard on the body. It also demanded a mental toughness.

Cultivating that toughness paid off now as he kept his expression impassive, showing no reaction to the news.

"I realize this isn't what you hoped to hear." The doctor's voice gentled. "I concur with your team specialist and the other physician you saw that the second injury to your ACL and playing while injured contributed to what we're seeing on the MRI. Surgery is not advised and, if done, would not give you the desired results."

Dustin had heard it all before. Still, he'd held out hope.

"Is there a chance you're wrong?" Dustin had never been one to give up easily. That tenacity and determination had served him well over the years. "Like I said, I'm willing to put in the work, do whatever—"

"I'm not wrong." Despite the firm tone, sympathy filled the doctor's pale blue eyes. "The fact that you've worked so hard on your rehab after the first surgery is why you were able to go back. Continuing to play after sustaining the second injury was a game changer."

As much as he wanted to return to his team, Dustin wouldn't go back and be less. His teammates, who wanted to win, deserved better.

Pushing to his feet, Dustin stuck out his hand. "I appreciate your time."

The doctor rose and gave his hand a firm shake. "You were an amazing player."

Were. Even the doctor was speaking in the past tense.

Dustin rode the elevator down to the main floor of the midtown office building, disappointment and grief battering at his control.

Helping his team win the Stanley Cup had been worth it, he reminded himself. Despite the positive thoughts, when he stepped outside, Dustin had to stop to catch his breath.

Hockey had been his life. The other players, his family. All that was gone now.

The irritating buzz of his phone had him setting his jaw in a hard line. If some reporter had gotten his private number…

Dustin jerked the phone from his pocket and glanced at the display. He took a steadying breath before he answered. "Hi, Dad."

"How did the doctor's visit go?" The carefully cultivated easy tone didn't fool Dustin. His father was as apprehensive about this visit as he'd been.

"Wallace concurs with the other two."

Silence for one, two, three long seconds.

"Perhaps there's someone else. I heard of a doctor in—"

"Dad. This guy was thorough." Dustin kept his tone matter-of-fact, understanding this news was nearly as devastating to his father as it was to him.

Hockey hadn't just been Dustin's life for the past twenty-plus years, starting with peewee leagues, it had been his father's life, as well.

"I'm sorry, son." Terry Bellamy cleared his throat, then spoke in a light tone. "What are you going to do? You are the Player with the Plan, after all."

The moniker the media had given Dustin early in his career

had stuck. He'd not only been a physical player, but he'd managed his emotions and kept his focus. He'd played smart. Not only on the ice, but in how he'd managed his career.

The six-year multimillion-dollar contract he'd signed shortly before his first injury had been one of the smartest.

"I'm considering several possibilities. Freddie and I will be discussing all my options in more depth."

His dad didn't push. From the time he'd been drafted at twenty-two, Dustin had been in charge of his career. With, of course, input from his agent, Freddie Wurtz.

"Your mom and I would love to have you home this Christmas."

"I have no doubt Ashleigh's boys will keep you both extremely busy." Dustin's sister had four kids under eight. His mom and dad doted on their grandsons.

"They'd love to see Uncle Dustin." His dad's tone turned persuasive. He obviously was not ready to give up without a fight.

Dustin had no doubt some of his tenacity came from this man, who'd been such a strong support all these years.

Which was why Dustin knew he needed a good reason not to go to Minnesota and spend Christmas with the family. Not wanting to deal with questions about his future wouldn't be considered an acceptable excuse.

"There's this woman I've been seeing." Dustin kept his tone casual. "I'm going to spend the holidays with her."

"Oh. Really?" His dad's voice held surprise. "You haven't mentioned anyone. You always said hockey and relationships are impossible together."

"That's what I thought." Dustin hadn't mentioned anyone, because there was no one to mention. But he couldn't deal with the family right now, so fictional girlfriend it was. "Thanks for all you've done, Dad. I couldn't have made it this far without you."

"You sound as if your life is over." Worry filled his dad's voice. "This is simply the beginning of a new chapter."

"It is." Dustin spoke with more confidence than he felt at the moment. "We'll talk later."

No longer the Player with the Plan, Dustin began walking and soon found himself at Rockefeller Center, gazing down at the skaters going around and around on the ice.

The tree and other signs of the approaching holiday season seemed a mockery of the sadness that held him in a stranglehold.

What am I going to do?

The grip on his chest tightened at the question.

He pulled out his phone, then realized he had no one to call. His best friends were also his teammates, and he wasn't ready to talk to them about this. Regardless of what he'd said to his dad, he also didn't want to deal with his agent. Not yet. And he couldn't call a girlfriend who didn't exist.

In this city of millions, Dustin suddenly felt very alone. His lavish hotel suite held no appeal. Besides, when he'd slipped out of the hotel this morning, he'd noticed a couple of sports reporters in the lobby.

He needed a place to lie low. A place to regroup. Most of all, a place that would give him the time and space necessary to come up with a plan.

To read the rest of this beautiful heartfelt story, pick up your copy of Home for the Holly Days now!

ALSO BY CINDY KIRK

Good Hope Series

The Good Hope series is a must-read for those who love stories that uplift and bring a smile to your face.

GraceTown Series

Enchanting stories that are a perfect mixture of romance, friendship, and magical moments set in a community known for unexplainable happenings.

Hazel Green Series

These heartwarming stories, set in the tight-knit community of Hazel Green, are sure to move you, uplift you, inspire and delight you. Enjoy uplifting romances that will keep you turning the page!

Holly Pointe Series

Readers say "If you are looking for a festive, romantic read this Christmas, these are the books for you."

Jackson Hole Series

Heartwarming and uplifting stories set in beautiful Jackson Hole, Wyoming.

Silver Creek Series

Engaging and heartfelt romances centered around two powerful families whose fortunes were forged in the Colorado silver mines.

Sweet River Montana Series

A community serving up a slice of small-town Montana life, where helping hands abound and people fall in love in the context of home and family.

Made in United States
North Haven, CT
29 November 2023

44745179R00139